RECKLESS
Abandon

HEATHER LEIGH

Jon,

thank you for being my number one fan, your support, drive and encouragement is what gets me through till the end of everything.

Sofia,

your little self amazes me each and every day, being a Mom has taught me so much in life.

My Family,

for letting me be me, and being patient with all of my takeovers.

Friends,

for the constructive criticism and positive reinforcements.

Readers,

for giving my books a chance and following me along this new journey.

Indie Authors,

for the advice, guidance and feedback

BURNING DESIRE

Condemned Angels MC Series, #1

Jeremy Moretti and Chase DeLuca have grown up together and into different MCs. Their lives were promised and destined to the Condemned Angels and Hell's Rebels. As they grew, so did Chase's feelings for Jeremy's younger sister, Roxanne.

Stemming from separate clubs, they have all the stakes against them. Michael Moretti, President of the Condemned Angels has forewarned Chase to stay away from his daughter. There is too much at risk and clubs stick to their own kind. No mixing whatsoever.

The years apart have done them good, however, Roxanne has finished school and is back home, and back in Chase's life. However, she isn't alone. Roxanne is dating the Treasurer of her father's club.

Things start to go wrong as their secret feelings grow stronger for one another. Will Chase fight for what has always been his, or will the MC stand in his way?

RIDE HARD

Condemned Angels MC Series, #2

Jeremy Moretti, son the of the Condemned Angel's President, has always had eyes for Nicole, his baby sister, Roxy's best friend.

Nicole has eyes for both Jeremy and Hunter.

The Condemned Angels MC is the only family Nicole has left. After a series of events that almost cost Nicole to take her own life, Jeremy was the one to save her.

They have both struggled with sexual frustration for years, and have been holding back on each other. Being too stubborn and hard headed, Jeremy decides it's best to push her away. When he doesn't step up to the plate, Hunter is there to break her fall.

While Hunter and Nicole's relationship blossoms, Jeremy tries to move on. But, yet, he can't let her go. It always been here, and it always comes back to Nicole.

After the death of the rival MC's President, Ryder, has the Devil's MC in an uproar as Ryder's surviving brother, Jax has come to seek revenge. With revenge, Jax brings unknown secrets that pertain to Nicole, which may risk everything, her safety, her MC family, and most importantly, Jeremy.

PRAISE FOR RIDE HARD

"Team Jeremy. Team Hunter. Heartbreak, destruction, suspense, dirty passionate love. Heather Leigh was serious with the title of this book - get ready to Ride Hard."
- **Deliciously Wicked Books**

"Hunter, JESUS, is to die for (DO YOU HEAR ME – I WANT HUNTER – I CLAIM HIM HE IS MINE). Hunter is caring, sweet, alpha and a totally dirty talking biker (THAT DOES THINGS TO MY INSIDES)."
- **Lustful Literature**

"Is Jeremy ready to tuck his big ton salami between his legs and finally admit what everyone knows that he loves Nicole and wants her badly? Will the truth that Nicole is smacked with ruin any and all relationships that she holds near and dear? And what the heck is that with Hunter, umm hello so did not see that in the walls..."
- **Sassy Girl Books**

"Heather Leigh does a good job creating drama and suspense to keep us entertained...well that's not all that kept me entertained...wink wink!"
- **iscreambooks**

"I was feenin for this book as soon as Burning Desire cliffed me, now I am foaming at the mouth waiting for book 3..."
- **We Stole Your Book Boyfriend**

"A lot transpires in this book. A lot of the story pulls together. Shocking revelations will keep you literally on the edge of your seat. I have enjoyed reading this series more than I though possible. I have been left wanting more after each book. Heather has written an amazing story with equally amazing characters. I can't wait to see what she has in store for book three!"
- **Love Between the Sheets**

"After the way Burning Desire was left I was gunning for this book and again I was not disappointed! I love MC books and I loved this book. Heather has done an amazing job."
–Eye Candy Book Store

"How long do I have to wait for the next one because I need it like yesterday? Great job keeping me interested and wanting, no wait strike that, NEEDING more!"
- Twinsie Talk

"Just like in the first book, this will have you sitting on the edge of your seat. My eyes were glued to the pages. It was hot, sexy, packed with action and some sexy tough badass bikers! What a twist to the story and holy fucking cliffhanger! Again, well done Heather Leigh for another fantastic book and I can't wait for the next one."
- Jennifer's Book Obsession

"*I* promise to *treat you* as good as my leather and *ride you* as much as my *Harley*."

– SONS OF ANARCHY

CHAPTER 1

HUNTER

NOTHING LIKE HAVING A FUCKIN' GUN POINTED AT YOUR HEAD. THERE WE WERE, knelt on our knees with our hands on the back of our heads.

"Fuck!" I roared out loud, while I shook my head from side to side. I was really fucked up, seeing Eva...after all these years. I didn't know what the fuck to think. I couldn't get the image of her out of my mind, even with a loaded gun pointed at my head.

"Hands behind your fucking backs!" a man yelled at us. Jeremy, Derrick and myself followed orders. With clenched jaws, we gradually obeyed. Our wrists were immediately zip-tied and dark fabric bags were thrown over our heads. I had no fucking clue how we got from point A to point B. Somehow I ended up on a chair in a room. At least I was still alive, fuckin'- A.

The bag was pulled from my head; and I immediately took a deep breath of fresh air. That fucking thing was suffocating my ass.

My eyes squinted under the bright light that hung over my head. I took in my surroundings, wood paneled walls, and a cement floor. The thing that stood out above the rest was the potent wave of chemicals or solvents that hung in the air. What the fuck? The door to the room that I resided in opened. Jax stood there, nodding to the Prospects to stand down as he entered.

"What the fuck were you three doing, spying on my fucking clubhouse? You boys have a death wish or some shit?" Jax said as he closed the door behind him. It was just the two of us. My hands were still tied behind my back, which fucking killed my shoulders. Being as built as I was and tied up didn't exactly work together. I straightened my spine while I pulled my shoulders and neck back faintly. I looked him square in the eye.

"You have Condemned Angel's property here that needs to be returned," I stated. I thought back to right before we were caught. Jax had taken Nicole upstairs, to what must have been his bedroom. A woman was waiting for them; as soon as she laid eyes on Nicole, she had taken an interest in her. Fucking eyed her up like she would be her next meal to devour. I'm all for girl on girl action but shit, that's when I took notice of the hair. It wasn't a ginger red, it was a 'hello, my hair is red as fuck' color. Long, thick curls of endless bright red laid down that girl's back. As soon as her face was visible, I couldn't believe my eyes.

It was Eva, my Eva, my wife.

past ...

"Hunter!" Eva called out as she tossed her keys onto the ceramic dish that sat by the front door.

"Yeah, babe?" I answered her, yelling from the kitchen.

"Mmm, something smells good!" She walked barefoot into the kitchen, wearing high-rise cut off jean shorts and a black tank top, which set off her new bright ass red hair. Eva had an obsession with Jessica Rabbit from the movie 'Who Framed Roger Rabbit', which led to the va-va-voom hair. It was up in a messy bun thing that chicks do, and her young face was beautiful as ever. Eva was about five years, give or take, younger than me.

"Chinese tonight, baby."

"My favorite!" She fished out a couple packets of duck sauce from drawer.

"I know." I grinned up at her. Little did she know what I had waiting for her at the end of our meal.

After we sat in the living room and finished our food, Eva sat back after unbuttoning her shorts. God, she was so damn sexy.

"Oh God, look away, baby. You don't want to see this." She giggled as she exhaled and let her imaginary gut out. Her flat belly rounded out with air, the roundness similar to being pregnant. Pregnant. I couldn't wait to see Eva waddling around with my baby inside of her. Whoa man, one thing at a fuckin' time.

"You know that shit just makes you even sexier? You giving me a hand with a head start on them shorts?" I crawled over to her with our favorite part of the meal, the fortune cookies.

"Oh, let me go first, baby?" Eva ignored my comment and immediately sat up and scurried herself to the edge of the couch. She sat perched there waiting. Like I was going to say otherwise to my girl? Fuck no.

"Always." I held up her fortune cookie to her.

"I don't get to pick?" She cocked her eyebrow.

"Fine, go for it." I held open my fist, full of fortune cookies sealed in individual plastic baggies.

"That's more like it!" Eva stuck out that little pink tongue, my fuckin' dick is already twitching. Easy, killer.

Our Chinese dinner traditions always ended with reading our fortunes out loud, and adding "in bed" at the end. This had made for some good memories, although, tonight's fortune was far different than any other.

"Read yours first!" Damn, bossy girl.

"Easy." I laughed while I cracked open my cookie. I already knew what the fortune said...every single cookie in my hand all read the same message. Thank God, I was prepared for that shit.

"Your many hidden talents will become obvious to those around you....in bed." I wiggled my eyebrows up at her, as she busted out laughing.

After she took a deep breath and wiped an escaping tear from her eye, Eva cracked open her cookie. She quickly read it to herself, and scrunched up her face.

"What's wrong? What does it say, baby?" I sat up on my knees and started to move towards her.

"This makes no sense."

"What? Let me see." I put out my palm to her, curling my fingertips for her to hand it over.

"See?" Eva was getting pissed about her fortune, the one I specifically had created for her.

"How doesn't it make sense?" I chuckled.

"Read it."

"'Will you marry me?'" I peeked up at her.

"See? That doesn't sound good with 'in bed' at the end of it!" Her small arms flailed about.

"Well, how about this? 'Will you marry me, Eva... in bed, forever, until our dying day?'" Eva suddenly looked down at me, as I was holding out a ring while on bended knee.

"Oh my God!" Her hands flew to her mouth as realization hit her, my pansy ass was proposing to her. For once, in all the time that I knew her, she was speechless.

"You going to leave me hanging here, baby?"

"Oh God! Yes!!!" Eva squealed, giving me her hand as her feet danced in place. As soon as that bad boy was on, I rose to my feet; my hands guided up the back of her thighs, and cupped her firm ass. Immediately, she jumped on me, and I caught her. Long, lean legs wrapped around my waist as her mouth attacked mine. Fuck, I love this woman. Eva damn near mauled my ass with kisses.

"Yes." Kiss "Yes." Kiss "Oh God, yes." Eva pushed her hot little cunt against my abs, and we were off to bed so I could lay claim on my Old Lady, the future Mrs. Sabatino.

present ...

"Why are you fucking smiling? You need to be fucking listening to me, mother fucker!" Jax's voice brought me back to the current situation, just as he smacked me across the face with the butt of his gun.

"Yes, what the fuck do you want, pussy?" I groaned as I spit a mouthful of blood onto the floor, and licked my cut lip.

"I asked you a question. What. The. Fuck. Are. You. Doing. Here?" Jax shouted the words in my face.

"First off, back the fuck up. Second, get a fucking mint. Third, you have Condemned Angel's property here."

"Jeremy and I already sorted that out. Nicole is a fair trade."

"Well, then why don't you talk to him about it?"

"Maybe a demonstration would be good for him," Jax chuckled as he turned and left the room I was in.

Shit.

CHAPTER 2

JEREMY

I KNEW THAT I HAD BEEN SEPARATED FROM HUNTER AND DERRICK RIGHT AWAY. I would have heard Derrick's ass complaining about some shit. Where I was held, it was quiet, too fucking quiet. I was sitting, my guess, on a chair. I knew that I was in the Devil's MC clubhouse, the faint bass of the music hit, vibrating the floor under my feet. So this meant I wasn't on a ground level. I heard the sound of a deadbolt unlocking, and heavy boots entering the room that I was in.

"Took you long enough, I'm getting lonely here," I shouted out to Jax, I knew he was there. I heard his deep laugh.

"You have no reason to be here, Moretti. We already discussed little Nikki." I hated that fucking nickname he'd given her.

"She doesn't belong here, or to you."

"Oh yes, she does. The fact that you're here as well, it's like a Condemned Angels BOGO sale."

"You have a problem with my club, my family, you talk to me. Not her. I'm fucking settling this shit."

"I can't let her go. She has responsibilities now in this club."

"Fuck that, like what? Being the MC's entertainment?"

"No, my personal entertainment." I strained against my restraints.

"I'll fucking kill you if you touch her, I swear it." My wrists and ankles were tied to the chair I was seated on, the plastic zip ties started to cut into my skin, but I couldn't have given two shits.

The door to the room opened again; there were scuffling footsteps and a pair of heels. The hood was ripped from my head; I quickly blinked to adjust myself to the dark room. The scene before me was that pesky redhead, holding Nicole by the back of her head. She knocked the back of Nicole's knee, which caused her legs to buckle from under her. Nicole fell forward onto her hands and knees; a cry escaped from her lips as her head was yanked back to look up at me.

"Nic." Her name rolled off my tongue, I didn't even realize it. Her big blue eyes watered as she was held in Eva's grip.

"Isn't that something? I have something you want, something that you love. Isn't that a coincidence?" Jax was eating this shit up.

"She belongs to me." My voice bounced off the walls of the room. Nicole's eyes went big, as if she couldn't believe I just laid my claim on her.

"He loves her." Eva face went soft and unreadable before curling into an evil grin. What was that shit about?

"Like I told you before, Nikki is Devil's property, no one else's. Do you want to know what it feels like to have something happen to someone you love?" Jax stepped up to Nicole, and I pulled my wrists further against the ties that were now drawing blood.

Eva stepped back, releasing Nicole, and Jax took over the grip on the back of Nicole's head. She was knelt before him, and Jax had a sickening smile splayed across his face.

"Get off me!" Nicole shouted, as a few tears fell from her eyes.

"Shut the fuck up!" Jax slapped her across her face, resulting in Nicole crying out; she let her head hang down, her hair curtained her face. I felt my veins bulge as I flexed my fists and my neck go hot as I yelled out loud.

Jax knelt down in front of Nicole; he swept her long hair aside, cupped her face, and raised her chin. The blood seeping from her freshly busted lip had me fucking livid. Jax's hold on her chin tightened as he tugged her face forward to his. He kissed her. Jax fuckin' kissed my Old Lady.

Nicole's sounds of struggle filled my ears. He finally pulled away after he fucking assaulted her mouth; his face was covered in her blood. Nicole spit in his face, and Jax handed out another slap across the face.

"Get the fuck off of her!"

Jax looked over his shoulder at me as he stood.

"Unzip my pants," Jax ordered Nicole, while he still held eye contact with me. *You gotta be fuckin' kidding me.*

"Hell fuckin' no! Fuck you!" Nicole yelled up at him from the ground.

I felt my jaw clench. This was a sick fucker.

"I said unzip them, bitch!"

Nicole's eyes shot over to me. I looked down at my lap, shook my head, and then looked back up at her. Fuck. She had no fucking choice. Nicole's small shaky hands unhurriedly rose to the front of Jax's jeans. The sound of his zipper had me clenching my jaw and breathing deeply through my nostrils.

"That's it," Jax coaxed her.

Nicole pulled out his dick from inside his pants. The sick fucker was already hard for his own sister. I'm going to fucking kill him. She went to say something, but hesitated.

"I know you are anything but shy, you better get your hot little mouth on my dick or your boyfriend dies." Eva started to walk over to where I sat, and stood behind me. I abruptly felt the cool metal barrel against the back of my head.

Nicole's eyes went dark, and she leaned forward, guiding her mouth to her hand that was currently resting on his dick. My eyelids shut right before she made contact.

"Christ, your mouth is made for sucking dick. I'm sure you already know that, Moretti," Jax's voice taunted me. I opened my eyes

8

to see Nicole staring at me while she proceeded to give him head. Motherfucker actually had the balls to hold her hair back so I could get the full effect.

Jax rapidly gripped a handful of her hair, which caused Nicole to wince in pain, and her eyes shot up to him.

"Eyes on me! Don't be pretending that you have his dick in your mouth. You're sucking *my* dick, bitch." A tear escaped the corner of her eye as she held eye contact with him. Jax's head fell back as he thrust his pelvis towards her face, causing her to gag. Nic's one hand shot to his thigh, trying to push him backwards to keep herself from gagging, but Jax kept her put.

"Fuck yeah baby, just like that. You're going to make me come so fucking hard, and you're going to swallow it all too." Just as he finished his sentence, the grip on Nicole's hair tightened as Jax shoved his dick further down her throat, getting his release. As soon as he pulled out of her mouth, Nicole sat back on her heels, and stuck her fingers down her throat. She threw it all up. Good girl.

"Take her out." Jax nodded to Eva as he tucked himself back into his pants.

Eva obeyed and gathered Nicole off the ground.

"Fuck you, I'm not leaving him." She struggled in Eva's arms.

"Nicole," I warned her.

"Better listen to your man, Nicole," Eva's said softly in her ear. My jaw clenched. Fuck, I just wanted to grab Nicole and take her away from this shit. Nicole glanced at me before shutting up and walking away.

THAT REDHEADED BITCH GUIDED ME BY MY CUFF-BOUND WRISTS TO A ROOM down the hall with no window. She shoved me down onto the bed by my shoulder.

"Fuckin' watch it, bitch!" I yelled up at her, while I shrugged her hand away from its current location.

"You better watch that smart ass mouth of yours, baby girl." She firmly held onto my jaw, while her eyes scanned my face. "So, which one are you fucking?"

"Excuse me?"

"Which one are you fucking, Jeremy or the other one? Or both?" She grinned down at me.

"What's it to you?" My chin jutted upward.

"Just curious to see if I can take one for a little joy ride, which one would you recommend?"

"Fuck you!" I spit up at her, but she jumped back in time to avoid getting hit.

Eva stepped back up to me, my head was pulled backwards and sharp pain ran over my scalp. *Fuck, I'm going to be bald by the end of this shit, I swear to God.*

"You. Will. Respect. Me. You. Little. Cunt." She yanked my hair back with each word.

I was silent. *Fuck you, bitch. Calling me a cunt? Ha, just you fucking wait.*

"There...that's better." Eva released her grip on my hair. "I'll go and make sure the boys have a proper welcoming to the Devil's clubhouse." Her chocolate-colored eyes sparkled with amusement. Her red-painted nails pushed a piece of hair behind my ear; she leaned down and kissed my lips. The blood rushed to my ears, adrenaline pumped through my veins. I kept completely still, watching her every move.

As Eva approached the doorway, she looked over her shoulder and called, "Maybe I'll even let you watch." She winked at me and left the room. I heard the sound of a deadbolt clicking into place.

I released the breath that I held in. My lungs burned. I was ready to fucking kill that bitch. I threw myself backwards onto the bed, and let out a frustrated scream.

CHAPTER 3

Eva

I QUICKLY LOCKED THE DOOR AFTER I EXITED THE ROOM, JUST AS JAX INSTRUCTED me to. I hope I was believable. If they knew who I really was, I would be six feet under. The Condemned Angels have been fucking my whole flow up. But, with them here, it will keep Jax distracted. Just as I was about to walk away, I heard Nicole yell out. Poor thing, she doesn't even know the half of it. Now, for the second part of my to-do list, check up on the other guys that came in with Jeremy. My stiletto heels clicked on the hardwood floor as I made my way down to the basement of the clubhouse. The smell of chemicals barely stung my nose; I was used to that shit.

I passed the room full of women wearing only their panties and bras. They wore surgical masks as they were cutting up bricks of cocaine. The girls only wore their skivvies so the dusting of cocaine in the air wouldn't be traced on their clothing. The Devils were smart, but not as smart as my boys.

There were a series of rooms in the back, dim-lit hallway. It gave me the fucking creeps being down here. The hallway light flickered as I searched for the key to my next stop. I swiveled the keys on the ring as I swung my hair over my shoulder. I stepped into the room, and a broad back and shoulders faced me. Big muscular arms were cuffed at the wrists behind his back. The sheer size of the man was stirring things up in my lady bits. *Focus, Eva.* Thick jean-clad thighs sat apart, and his head full of dark hair was hung low. *Asleep. Fucking figures.*

"Wakey, wakey!" I slammed the door shut and his head shot upwards, resulting in a groan of pain.

"Fuck off." His voice sounded sexy as hell.

"That's no way to speak to an Old Lady." I started to walk around to face him. His head sluggishly rose.

"Or do you mean, it's no way to speak to my wife?" Hunter made eye contact with me.

I gasped as my hand shot to my chest, I was in shock.

"Hunter. What the fuck are you doing here?" I said in a voice just above a whisper, I glanced upward to confirm the door was closed.

"I should be asking you the same fuckin' question, Eva." He raised his square chin; I saw the muscles working on his jawline.

"Please tell me that this isn't real, that this isn't fucking happening." I started to pace. Don't think I missed Hunter's eyes traveling over my body. My black bandage-styled dress fit me like a second skin, and I knew I looked good in it. He must have taken a liking to his new view.

"You look like you got yourself into a real fine mess." Hunter winced in pain trying to adjust his shoulders. "A little help?"

"Are you serious?" I stopped in my tracks and slapped a hand on my upper thigh, frustrated as hell.

"It's the least you can do, considering..." he trailed off and his dark eyebrows shot upward.

"Shhh, don't you even fucking think it. You trying to get me killed?" I rushed to sort through the keys for the small one I was looking for. Pulling at the hem of my dress, I crouched down behind him, fumbling with the lock. I tried to avoid touching his hands, but that went out the window as I unlocked the cuffs. His skin was hot, and he smelled the exact same as I remembered, like cedar and man. *Don't ask me what man smells like, but it's fucking delicious. God, he looks good. Damn him!*

"Me? Are you trying to get yourself killed? Don't you remember our last conversation?" Hunter was pissed. *Of course I fuckin' remembered.* That night my heart broke, I lost everything we ever had, I lost the love of my life.

"Yes," I stated, as I released the cuffs from his wrists. I didn't expect him to move so quickly. He shot out of the chair, knocking me back on my ass. Before I knew it, he had me pinned to the cold cement floor as he straddled my hips. One hand rested on my throat and the other gathered my wrists above my head. I thrust my hips upwards against his.

"Then what the fuck are you doing here? With him?" Hunter shouted in my face.

"You know exactly why." I stared up at him with glossy eyes.

HUNTER

CHRIST, I NEARLY FORGOT HOW GOOD SHE FELT UNDERNEATH ME. SHE LOOKED fucking stunning. That bright ass red hair was splayed out all around her, checks flushed and her big tits nearly spilling out of her tight dress.

"You had the opportunity to get out, Eva." I pushed down on her wrists.

"I know that! I didn't have a choice. After all the shit we had, I had dirty hands, and this is me cleaning them." She looked me square in the eye as if to challenge me.

"Fuck!" I shouted in her face, and she flinched; the long hair beside her face blew over her neck and down her chest. My eyes followed the strand.

"My face is up here, you know?" I smiled wide.

"Not the first time you've told me that." I leaned closer to Eva, her breathing all of a sudden got deeper, pushing her perfect tits closer to me. *Fuck.* My mind drifted to that first night when Eva and I met, when our shit storm began.

past ...

I had been with Hell's Rebels, celebrating my patch-in at the local strip club, Bottom's Up.

Eva was waitressing that night, I can't imagine what she saw in me, but something that night was the spark that ignited it all.

The boys and I had just arrived at Bottom's Up, we got comforttable for an entire night's worth of celebrating, entertainment, and definitely some pussy pounding afterward. We settled into the plush red velvet couches that circled the base of the stage, Chase already had a few waitresses at our beck and call. One of them being Eva. Hell yes, I looked the girls over- picking my pussy for the night. Rubbing my hands together, my eyes did all the work. Fuck, if I wasn't Hunter and the Three Bears tonight. The first was too skinny for my liking; the second chick was too tall.

Then, there was small but mighty Eva. She stood there, arms crossed, wearing the club uniform of black thigh-high boots, black fishnet stockings that led to her black leather booty-shorts and a matching cropped leather halter top, that made her tits look fucking amazing. Eva had the radiance of a fucking goddess with her dark eyes, thick lashes, olive skin, and full lips that I was already picturing around my dick. What I would guess as full D-cup sized breasts, toned abs and killer fucking legs rounded out the goddess package. Damn, didn't her just standing there, looking pissed as all hell, make my dick hard. She watched as I drank her body in.

"I have a fucking face, you know!" Eva said in a hard tone. She uncrossed her arms, and placed them on her perfect hourglass shaped hips. It took a second for me to register that she was actually talking to me, and with such disrespect. That was the moment when I knew I was fucking doomed because I wanted her, *BAD*. "It's up here!" She pointed her finger upwards, but I was still too focused on the middle parts of her.

"Oh, I like this one." I darted my tongue out and licked my bottom lip. I watched her eyes flicker down to my mouth. No reaction on her face. Odd, that never happens. She will make this fun tonight.

"'This one is off limits, I'd rather go blow my brains out than be caught up with you, biker boy." Eva formed her two fingers and her thumb into a gun and pointed that said "gun" at her own temple. She pulled the "trigger" and laughed as she flung her then dark brown hair over her shoulder.

Goddamn, I loved me some good chasing.

"Yeah, why don't you get that stick out of your ass, and then I can replace it." I smirked up at her scowling face, and the MC brothers were laughing their asses off. They knew me too well; Eva was just my type.

As she opened her mouth, a veteran server cut Eva off.

"That's enough, Eva. You don't ever disrespect the club like that again, do you understand me?"

"You're going to be the lucky lady that takes care of me tonight, Eva." I fucking loved the way her name tasted on my tongue. I could only imagine how good she would taste. Her chest expanded with the deep breaths she took. Eva spun on her heel and walked away from the group. Goddamn, did I mention that ass? I bet I could bounce quarters off that bad boy.

Within the next ten minutes, I had tucked a couple singles into the G-string of some chick's ass. The stripper that was currently shoving her tits in my face offered me my first "patch-in" private dance.

"I don't normally do private dances, but for you...," the curvy blonde whispered into my ear, "I'd give you one hell of a show, baby." I felt her bare tits graze my arm as she pulled away. Just as I was about to respond, a small hand with a beer bottle slammed down on the table next to me, beer splashed up onto my arm and the topless dancer in front of me.

"What the fuck, Eva!" the broad screeched as she wiped her hands over her tits.

"Oh please, Ruby, like you didn't just give a private dance fifteen minutes before they arrived? Plus your little shows aren't all that you think they are. It wouldn't be 'one hell of a show' for him, guaranteed. You couldn't even give me a lady boner." Eva smirked, popping that curvy hip out, and rested the brim of her serving tray on my table.

"Fuck you, you little cunt!" The fucking claws came out. Fuck yes, someone get the pool of Jell-O ready!

"Ladies." I started to rise out of my seat. "Did you just say lady boner? " I laughed while shaking off my wet hand.

"I'm telling Reese." Little blondie stood and rushed to the back.

"Fuck," Eva grumbled under her breath as she grabbed her tray off my table. I grabbed the brim of the tray closest to me, forcing her body to jerk back in front of me.

"You just spilled beer all over me, sweetheart." I tightened my grip as Eva tried to tug back the tray. Like her small ass could do something.

"Fuck you. I'm not your sweetheart. You think you guys can just roll on in here 'cause you have your little fuckin' patches sewn onto your little Girl Scout vests and think you're God's gift to women. I say, 'fuck that shit'."

I released my grip, only to grab the part of the tray that was firmly planted against Eva's chest, right below her full breasts. She wasn't expecting that, and lost her balance. Eva stumbled in her heels in my direction, her lips parted as if to say something, but I beat her to the chase.

"You listen and you listen good. These patches protect your sorry ass and this fucking town. Why don't you show some fucking respect?" Her eyebrow cocked as she looked up at me. If I didn't know any better, she looked as if she enjoyed me talking to her like that.

"Fuck you, biker boy," Eva managed to say through gritted teeth. I pulled the tray away from her. Eva had glanced down, as if to realize her safety net just disappeared. I gripped her wrist and pulled her towards the bar. Reese stood behind the bar, stacking clean glasses. She had quickly glanced up to scope out the floor, and then back down for a second before her head immediately shot back up to see me dragging Eva beside me.

"We need a private room, NOW," I roared.

"The fuck we do, get your hands off me!" Eva pushed against my arms. Good thing I wore a sleeveless shirt under my cut tonight. My tribal tattooed sleeves were on display, and Eva's hot little hands splayed over my wide biceps.

Reese just grabbed me a key from under the bar, and tossed it to me without question.

"REESE!" Eva yelled over her shoulder as I led us down the back hallway.

I glanced at the key to see the room number and stopped at a room with a metal three on the door. I used one hand to unlock it. As soon as I had that shit opened, I tossed Eva's ass in there. She gained her balance on her tall heels. I need to fuck her in those...now.

"I swear to God, you don't want to fuck with me right now, biker boy."

"I'm no boy, baby. I can assure you of that. You have one hell of a fuckin' mouth on you, little girl." I pushed her to sit down on the leather couch. I liked being rough with her, 'cause I knew a bad bitch like her could take it.

"So fuckin' what?" Eva attempted to stand, and I pushed her back down by her shoulder. Her eyes narrowed up at me.

"You ready to apologize to me?" I took a step closer to her, Eva's head tipped back and she kept eye contact with me.

"I believe the question is, are you ready to apologize to me?" Her hands gripped the edge of the cushion on the couch.

"Ha, baby, you got it all twisted." I rubbed my hand down the short beard on my chin.

"You 'MC guys' are all the same." She did cute little air quotes.

"Meaning?"

"Meaning, you're all fucking assholes." She crossed her arms, and looked away from me. That's when it hit me; she must have had some beef with a brother of some sorts.

"What's his name?"

"Excuse me?" Her brown orbs found mine.

"Who has your panties up in a bunch?"

"Had."

"Say what?" I walked over to the wet bar and poured us both a bourbon on the rocks.

"Who had my panties up in a bunch?" She emphasized the past tense in her statement.

"Oh...in the past, huh? What happened, did he hurt your sensitive little girl feelings? Poor Eva." I mocked her in a sweet baby voice.

"Fuck off." Eva went to stand again, but I denied her of that. I pressed down on her bare shoulder to keep her ass planted there.

"Wrong answer." I took a seat next to her.

"Go to hell." She turned her body away from me. Bingo.

"Nope." I touched the glass to her bare arm. Eva looked down at it, before taking it and throwing back a mouthful of the amber-colored liquor.

She ran the back of her hand over her lips; pouty lips that I knew were burning from the alcohol.

"Why do you fucking care, huh? Aren't you just here for some tits and ass being shoved in your face, before taking home whichever pussy you want?"

"Is that what you want to happen?"

"Oh no, I don't think so. I'm not playing that game." Eva pushed the empty glass to the center of my chest.

"What game, Eva?" I grabbed her wrist. She tried to tug it back, but I held my grip on her delicate wrist. I placed her empty glass on the table beside the couch. I fished out an ice cube with three of my fingers.

"What are you doing?" She tried to look over my shoulder.

"Shut up for two fucking seconds." I ran the melting cube over the inside of her wrist, rubbing it in small circles. Hearing Eva's hiss from the cold meeting her skin was music to my ears. I sluggishly blinked, then looked up at her. I lowered my mouth and pulled the ice away at the same time. My lips came in contact with her wrist. I flicked my hot tongue against her cold skin. The goose bumps spread across her forearm. Eva's face softened, and her eyelids shut with a slow blink as she exhaled. Got her!

I kept my eye on her as I gave her a nip on the inside of her wrist. I did it hard enough to make her gasp and jump at the same time. My intention was to do it hard enough for it to leave a mark, and so she'd remember who put it there.

"Ready?"

"For what?" Eva jerked on her arm but I didn't let go. I pulled her small hand down to the crotch of my jeans, so she could feel exactly what I thought of her.

"To apologize." Her gaze fell to her hand's current location, on my dick.

Pulling her free hand back she shoved me backwards so I was flush against the back of the couch. *Oh fuck!* Eva seductively started to crawl in my lap. Her shoulder blades worked their way up and down like a lioness. She gripped the cushions on the back of the couch on either side of my head. I spread my legs, wide enough for her to straddle my one thigh. I could feel her heated little cunt through her thin shorts. *Oh hell yes, she wants this dick.*

The next thing I knew her lips were on my earlobe. She took it between her full lips and sucked until my lobe was between her teeth. My hands ran up the back of her stocking clad thighs, and rested on the round mounds of Eva's ass.

"If you ever put my hand on your dick again, without my consent, I'll fucking cut it off myself," she hurriedly whispered into my ear before shoving her bent knee into the family jewels. Eva stood over me, while I cupped my balls in pain, and cursed her the fuck out. Satisfied with herself, she fluffed her hair and walked out on me. I believe I just found the woman who is destined to be my Old Lady, fuck me.

CHAPTER 4

HUNTER

"GET THE FUCK OFF ME, HUNTER." EVA BROUGHT ME BACK TO THE PRESENT AS she forced her gaze to the side of the room. She avoided eye contact with me.

"And what exactly would you do? I'm guessing your Old Man doesn't know who you really are yet? Or are you just waiting for him to fall in love with you before you dick him over too? You are good at ruining people." Her eyes shut tightly, and her jaw tightened.

"Fuck you." Her voice sounded uneasy. I knew the effect I had on her. Eva was my greatest accomplishment. She learned to submit to me, and in return for her trust, I gave her my heart. *Fucking pussy-whipped.*

"Fuck me? That's the fucking thanks I get for trying to save your ass?"

I released her hands and gripped her jawline, forcing her to look at me, my other hand still on her throat. I saw the first tear escape the corner of her eye. I absent-mindedly stroked the column of her neck with my thumb to try and soothe her.

"Get off me!" She struggled. Eva pushed her heels into the ground and tried to buck me off with her hips. "You have no rights to me anymore." Hearing her say those words was like another fuckin' swift kick to the balls.

"You still have my last name, so yeah- I do have a fucking right."

"You made me leave!"

"After I fucking found out who you really were!" I shouted in her face.

"So what?"

"SO WHAT? That's all you have to say? You should be someone else right now, somewhere else. Married, living in a big house with a white picket fence with kids running around and a baby on your tits."

"That's cute and all but is that really what you thought I'd go and do? I can't just end my life and change what I do."

"Oh yeah, I know that, Eva. You made that clear when you made your decision that night. So, I took matters into my own hands and ended it. Before you got in too deep." I squeezed her jawline.

"Hunter...," she held onto my hand that rested on her throat, "if you don't stop..." Her face flushed. Either Eva was pissed or turned on. I'm siding with the latter of the two since we used to have hot make-up sex after a fight. Rarely, did we make it through the fights in their entirety. Maybe we fought for the sex. *Focus, Hunter.*

"You'll do, what?"

"It's what I won't be able to stop doing, is what I'm worried about." Her rich brown eyes bore into mine. More like, searched for something in mine. I could read her like a book, and she was longing. Longing for me. *Oh not this time, baby girl.*

Nicole

I MUST HAVE FALLEN ASLEEP AS SOME POINT. MY BODY JOLTED UPWARDS OFF THE small bed. My head had a dull ache from my hair being pulled. That fucking bitch! I winced as my fingertips massaged my scalp. I licked my dry lips, tasted the dried blood in the corner of my mouth, the same mouth that was wrapped around Jax's...oh God. I felt a dry heave working its way through my body.

JEREMY

WATCHING NICOLE WALK OUT OF THE ROOM, FUCKING KILLED ME. THE LOOK in her eyes will haunt me. The fact that Jax disrespected her, touched her, fuckin' A. I couldn't even think it without my blood pressure rising. I had to get us out of this situation, and fucking fast. The brothers have to realize we are missing and come looking for us sooner or later. I can only pray that they will come here.

Nicole

I WAS HALF SURPRISED TO FIND THAT THE ROOM I WAS BEING HELD IN HAD A bathroom. I rushed through the doorway to take the longest pee in the history of America. I avoided the mirror that hung on the wall, I didn't want, nor did I need to see the hot mess I was. I felt dirty, filthy from what Jax made me do. I didn't even want to picture the fucked up shit he had in store for me. But now that Jeremy, Hunter and Derrick are here, who the fuck knows what will happen. If Jeremy had only listened, and let me handle shit, we'd be all right and Jeremy would be safe.

Leaving the Condemned Angels wasn't something I wholeheartedly wanted to do, but it was something that needed to be done. I have grown up and into that MC, those men are my family. Hell, I grew up with Roxy, and there wasn't a moment I couldn't remember without them. When shit hit the fan with my Mom and

Dad, Moretti was there for me. In fact, the entire MC family was there for me. Hospital visits from when I OD'd, rehab was arranged and paid for, visitors every weekend, holidays, graduation- I had the entire group there. They had multiple chapters come in to see Roxy and I in our cap and gowns. They've seen me grow, fall, recover, and succeed.

Jeremy had saved me from myself, and for that, I owed it to him, his family, and the MC to do the right thing and give myself over. I wasn't going to let my sperm donor ruin my true family. They were all I had left in this world. A hard pounding at my door abruptly interrupted my thoughts. Before I knew it, the door swung open.

"Nikki?" I heard Jax sing out into the tiny room. *In here, you stupid motherfucker.* Sighing, I took a deep breath and met him in the bedroom.

"What do you want?" I grumbled at him, crossing my arms across the front of my body, feeling incredibly uncomfortable after today's earlier events.

"I have something for you." My heart jumped and my pulse sped up. *Jeremy?*

"Awe, look at how cute you look, thinking I actually brought you something you wanted."

"Fuck off." I turned my back to him. Jax's heavy boots clunked on the floor as he made his way to me. I felt his body so close to mine, his large frame against my petite body. My hair was swept away from my neck, and over my other shoulder, exposing my neck to him.

"Don't be mad at me." His tattooed hand gripped my waist and his lips hit the curve of where my neck and shoulder met. I shrugged away from him and rotated on my heel.

"Fuck you. Don't touch me, you sick fuck! I'm your sister, for cryin' out loud!" I sneered at him.

"So fucking what? Nina and I, we are very close. You and I may be related in some way or another, but Christ, look at you!" His vibrant blue eyes scanned my body.

"Fuckin' disgusting. What about your Old Lady? Doesn't she get jealous when you fuck your sister on the side?"

"Nah, it's an agreement we have and that she respects. Maybe your Old Man has the same agreement with you?"

"Ha, you're funny. That's the biggest fucking joke I've ever heard." I laughed out loud, only to have Jax push me up against the bathroom door. I squared my body up to his.

"You're a Devil now, the only Old Man you'll have is me. So you're going to see a whole new kind of world, little girl." Jax roughly cupped my cheek as he slowly licked my lips. I had to fight to keep the bile down in my throat. He released his grip and trailed his hand down the side of my body, palming my left breast, and jiggling it roughly.

"God damn, you taste so sweet, so innocent. I can't wait to fucking ruin you." Jax chuckled as he turned and walked away from me. "Oh, and by the way, Eva will be by to give you clothes, you'll be performing tomorrow. Get your rest, because you'll have one hell of an audience." The door slammed behind him, causing me to jump.

"Fuck." My head hung as tears burned my eyes. *I want to go home.*

CHAPTER 5

HUNTER

I STARED INTO HER EYES, I COULD SEE RIGHT THROUGH HER FACADE. MY EVA wasn't stupid enough for this shit. A woman of her stature, and ranking- it didn't add up. I took a deep breath; her sweet perfume coated my nostrils. She still wore the same perfume. *Fucking focus, she means nothing to you! She's a traitor and has lied before and she will do that shit again, don't fucking trust her.* I told myself, as I further scanned her face. My body was fighting me; it remembered just how good Eva felt below me. I slammed my palm against the floor by her head, which caused her to jump. Her small hands shoved at my chest.

"Not as strong as I remember," I whispered in her face, her baby hairs floated away from her temples.

"Fuck you." Eva's cheeks grew red with frustration.

"You already did that, in more ways than one. You going soft, Eva?" I saw the fire burn in her eyes, and her teeth clench.

"I said, fuck you! Get the fuck off me, you piece of shit." *God, she's so damn sexy when she's pissed.*

"Why, all of a sudden you have a change of heart?" I let her up. I caught a glimpse of her black lace panties, and new ink displayed on the backs of her upper thighs. Little bows tattooed right under that apple- shaped ass of her. *Fuck me.*

"You're so fuckin' confusing. Always playing mind games, Hunter. If you know what's good for you, you'll keep your mouth shut. Do us both a favor, and do what Jax wants and get the fuck out of here. Forget you even saw me." Eva's hand was on the lock of the door.

"Me, confusing? How about you?" I was somehow letting her get the best of me. I was pissed, and her change of pace put me over the top.

"Care to explain?" She released the lock, slowly turned to me, and took her stance with arms crossed.

"Two seconds ago you're eye-fucking the shit out of me, and taking me down ole' memory lane. Now, you're all "badass", and think you can fuckin' boss me around? Telling your husband to listen to your Old Man?" I backed her up against the metal door. Her eyes narrowed, and her cheeks flushed. I knew she was pissed.

"The reason I'm all "badass", is that I have a fuckin' rep to uphold here, Hunter. I'm sleeping with your enemy! We've been done and over since that day you made me leave. We have nothing further to talk about here. The longer I stay in this room, the greater the chances are of you giving me up. I have a job to do here, and you're not a part of it this time." She was stern with her words, trying to fuckin' hurt me. I couldn't deny the tightening in my gut when she admitted she was sleeping with Jax.

"One- I didn't make you leave, I allowed you to leave- alive. Two- I just want to get the fuck out of here alive, and will do so, when I have what we came for. Three- is what's between your legs getting the job done for you?" I yelled at her, louder with each thing I was ticked off on my fingers.

va

My blood boiled at his words. My right hand immediately shot up and slapped him across his face. We stood there breathing hot air into each other's faces. His raked his teeth over his bottom lip, then looked me square in the eye. Those dark eyes of his zoned in on my mouth. My lips parted with my heavy breathing. Before I knew what happened, Hunter's mouth crashed down onto mine, and my arms flung around his neck. His large hands circled my waist and pulled me into him. I stepped on just the balls of my feet in my sky-high heels, and pushed upward, closer to Hunter's mouth. It was as if we had never skipped a beat. My ass slammed against the door as he roughly pinned me with his body. Our kiss was aggressive, raw, sensual and stimulating. My body hummed against his. Every feeling, thought, and memory from our past relationship engulfed me. Hunter was, and still is, my addiction. Goddamn him. *Oh shit, what the fuck am I doing?*

I immediately forced my hands between our bodies. My hands rested on Hunter's well-built chest. I had to refrain from feeling the rest of his rock hard body as I pushed Hunter away and pulled my face away from his. A groan fell from his mouth as his eyes gradually opened. Our chests rose and fell as we both tried to catch our breath.

"What the fuck are we doing?" I whispered, my focus was on his full bottom lip, which was now deliciously swollen, thanks to me.

"The fuck if I know."

"It was nothing; we'll just forget it happened. I should go." I tried to tame my wild hair and licked my lips before rubbing them together. I still tasted him as my tongue darted out.

"You're right; it is and always will be nothing." He sounded offended, and tried to cover it up with his temper. Hunter pushed off the door, and my gaze hit the floor between us. I half expected him to finish what we started. Walking back to his metal seat, he sat there, just as I had found him minutes before- hands behind his back, facing away from me. My heart dropped into my stomach. I rapidly slapped the cuffs on Hunter's wrists. *How could I have been so stupid?*

"Isn't this just fucking ironic? You've probably been dying to do that since we've met." His voice was cold, and disconnected. I ignored his comment, and the painful ache in my heart.

"Well, since it's like that, you should know that your girl has been taken a liking to." I tightened his cuffs.

"My girl?" He looked at me sideways with an eyebrow cocked.

"Nicole." I already knew that she was Jeremy's but I just had to confirm since she didn't earlier.

"She was never fully mine." It stung to hear that she was anything with him. "That's Jeremy's Old Lady. So Jax better watch the fuck out."

"Well, then it will be refreshing to see someone fight for their Old Lady." *Low blow, Eva.*

"Eva, let's not even go there. You're right, you should go."

"I know that I'm right. Jax is waiting for me." I left him with that, and slammed the door shut. I leaned against the wall in the hallway and inhaled a deep breath, trying to soothe my nerves. I raised my trembling hands to my face as the memory of our last night together flooded into my mind.

CHAPTER 6

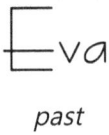va

past

I PULLED MY FORD EXPLORER INTO THE DRIVEWAY. I WAS DOING MY NIGHTLY
routine at the gym- cardio, weight lifting, and then yoga stretches. I
kept myself in great shape, per my true career; I had to keep myself in
tip-top shape without leading Hunter on. I reached under the driver
seat and made sure my 9mm was stowed away in the secret
compartment, and I was on my way inside.

"Babe, I'm-" My sentence fell short on my lips as I saw our home
in complete shambles. My bags immediately fell from my hands and
crashed to the floor. Everything was torn apart, picture frames on the
walls had either fallen or were crooked, coffee and end tables were
overturned in the living room. The broken lampshade projected light
up on the walls. Slowly, I proceeded further down the hallway. My
breathing became shallow and goose bumps broke out over my skin.
The framed pictures in the hallway that led to the kitchen were

unrecognizable. Broken glass crunched beneath my sneakers, one of the first pictures that had been taken of us at a clubhouse BBQ was shattered and smeared with blood. *Oh God, no.*

My heart slammed against my rib cage. He knows. It was my initial thought, my worst nightmare come true. My breath hitched as I stood in the doorway to the kitchen. Papers, that I recognized from my "thick-as-shit" file on the Hell's Rebels, had now been thrown about the kitchen. Blood smeared the pages that I had spent two years gathering—photographs, payroll books, blueprints, license plate numbers, background checks, passports, and more. My badge and ID tag sat on top of the heap. Looking up, I saw the cap to the Jack Daniels bottle sitting on the countertop. A few broken glasses sat in the sink. This is not good. My heart sunk into my stomach, and then I heard shuffling. *Hunter.*

"Oh good, you're home," I heard Hunter's slurred words call out to me. Panicked, my eyes went to the knife block- empty. I tiptoed to the cabinet above the refrigerator, grabbing the box of honey nut Cheerios; I immediately knew the box felt too light to be hiding my .38 caliber. Fuck!

"There she is." Clapping, Hunter stumbled into the kitchen doorway that connected to the den he used as a man cave. I immediately spun on my heel, and held onto the refrigerator door to keep myself upright.

"Let me give you a-round-of-fuckin'-'plause for your wonderful performance. You had us all fuckin' fooled."

"Hunter." His name fell from lips on a sigh. I took the image of him in. His 6'2" muscular body swayed. He was wearing one of his signature outfits, a black crew cut t-shirt, dark-wash jeans, and black Timberland boots. The laces were undone on his boots, the jeans hung dangerously low on his hips, and he had hell in his eyes. The neck of the empty Jack bottle was tucked tightly in the crook of his elbow. I could see the dried blood on his knuckles as the last clap echoed throughout the kitchen. Hunter's thick, tattooed forearms flexed as my eyes made their way to Hunter's face. Dark circles surrounded his bloodshot eyes. The neck of the bottle slid into the palm of his hand.

"Don't you even fucking say my name!" Hunter roared as he threw the empty bottle at me. I rapidly rolled to my right, avoiding the hit as the glass bottle exploded against the stainless steel surface of the fridge. My left arm rose and I tried to shield myself from the flying shards. He was on me in a second; I didn't even have time to react. Strong, calloused hands wrapped their way around my throat, my hands grabbed onto his wrists as I was brought to my tiptoes.

"Please!" I gasped out as hot tears streamed down my face. I needed to tell him the truth before he did this.

"You FUCKING liar!" Hunter roared loudly in my face. I felt his spit against my face; his temper caused him to shake me roughly.

"Let me explain," I choked out as I clawed his hands.

"Explain how you snuck your way into my MC, spied on my brothers and me, made me fall for you, I told you shit about my club, me, we're fucking married for Christ sakes- is that even real?"

"Yes! It all is. Hunter," his grip loosened somewhat as I tried to get my words out, "Hunter, I'm a federal agent. I was sent here to go undercover, to get to know your club, the Intel, get the inside on how you guys make your money. They thought Hell's Rebels were trafficking weapons, guns, drugs, you name it-"

"We don't do that shit!" he yelled at me, thrusting my back into the hard surface again.

"And, I know that! I was proving you innocent. I just didn't think that I'd fall for you during my time here. I did, and this is where it's led us, and yes- I'm your Goddamn wife! For-fucking-real." My voice held a raspy tone as he re-tightened his grip on my neck.

"You lied to me. How am I supposed to think that what you're saying right now is true? You lied, you're a disgrace to my MC, what we have...had, is a fuckin' joke." Hunter paused, his eyes closed slowly before he opened them again to look at me with sadness and disgust.

"I love you, Hunter. You have to believe me," I begged him as I winced in pain as his left hand left my throat and gripped my jawline.

"I don't have to believe anything you say. I don't feel anything for you, Eva. If that is even your real name?" Hunter's words hit me like a physical blow to the gut. I couldn't even hold back my tears. My entire world was falling apart right before me. I was in so deep with the MC that I grew attached to them. They were my family, my only family that I knew of. Going undercover meant me gaining a family, people who loved me, or at least the idea of me. Hunter's deadly gaze was easing up, as he was wearing down; his red eyes were brimming with tears. He was fighting a battle all on his own.

"You and the MC are all I have, Hunter. Fuck my job, I don't care anymore- this is us. You and me, that's all I care about." My eyes searched his for a reaction, something, anything.

"Oh, now you want it all, don't you?" Hunter yelled into my face. I'd never seen him like this before.

"I've never stopped wanting you! I can't deny who I really am."

"Who you want to be," he corrected me.

"What?"

"You fucking heard me. You're a poser, wanna-be, fake, phony, floozy, whatever you want to call it. You're it, because you'll never have this life again. I don't even know how you're still breathing right now. For what you have done, you should be dead!" Hunter's voice rose as the grip on my neck got tighter. My face heated as my knees slowly buckled. I clawed at Hunter's already bloodied hands.

"Baby," I barely got out as I saw the first tear escape his eye. My legs went out from underneath me; Hunter resumed his position as my body fell to the ground. He straddled my torso, bent on his knees above me, strangling the life out of me. He quickly glanced down at my hands, spotting my wedding ring, and a sob broke through his gritted teeth, and his hands suddenly dropped to the ground. *Thank you, Jesus!*

I gulped air into my now burning lungs, which put me in a coughing fit. As soon as I made eye contact with Hunter, I cupped his head that was now bowed down, resting on my chest. Slowly, I pulled his heavy head up. Hunter's face was now full of pain; teardrops fell from his dimpled cheeks, and onto my chest.

"I can't...I fuckin' love you too damn much to kill you." His confession stilled my heart. I didn't know what to say; all that was left was to do. Gently wiping away the sweat and tears from his face with the bottom of my tank top, I sat up on kitchen floor. Hunter sat back on his haunches, his shoulders rolled forward; the look of defeat was the very definition of how he looked. I knelt up onto my knees in front of him, our kneecaps touching. I was in love with the man who almost just killed me by asphyxiation. *I'm fucking fucked.*

I know the alcohol played a part in his emotional display, but I'd never seen him like this. Broken. I stroked back his hair, and pulled him up to face me; Hunter now straightened up onto his knees, my head had to tip back so that I could see the man I loved. My eyes roamed his face, first his eyes, then his lips. Hunter was doing the same to me; the tension between us could have been cut with a knife.

"Then don't..." I trailed off as Hunter's lips came crashing down onto mine. I pressed my body flush with his. As he groaned I opened my mouth, welcoming him into me. Hunter's large hands trailed down my back, and cupped my ass. Eager, he lifted me up, and my legs wrapped around his waist. As Hunter held onto me, he pushed off the ground one leg at a time, with me latched onto the front of his body. Stumbling in the hallway, Hunter bumped my back into the wall as he stumbled over fallen picture frames. I tore my mouth away from his as I leaned back and ripped my tank and sports bra over my head.

Growling, Hunter dipped his head down, and latched onto my neck, and made his way down south. I squeezed my thighs together, unable to ignore the zing I felt in my clit. Tingles spread throughout by body. No one could do me like Hunter; he made my body feel things that were unimaginable.

"I need you," I groaned as I felt his warm lips take hold of my right nipple. I yelped out in pleasure as he bit down on my sensitive bud.

"Hold on, baby, Hunter's got you," he soothed me as my hips tried to buck against his. Somehow we made it to our bedroom, our sanctuary.

HUNTER

YOU GOT TO BE FUCKING KIDDING ME. SHE WANTS A MAN WHO WILL FIGHT for her? She had that and fuckin' blew it being a FED.

CHAPTER 7

HUNTER

(past)

I DON'T KNOW HOW WE GOT HERE, BUT WE WERE. ONE SECOND I HAD HER ON the floor with just seconds to spare, and then in the next the sparkle of her wedding ring caught my attention. Then, I thought of our vows we told each other that day. I couldn't. Eva is everything I am. I fuckin' live for this woman. The mother to our future kids. I didn't have the fucking balls to do it. One last time, it's what we both needed.

As soon as I felt her warm hands on my face, I was a goner. Fuck me, how did she look so beautiful after I choked the shit out of her. My handprints glowed red and angry on her neck. How is she still standing right here in front of me, instead of running away? She's fucking stupid, and so am I. When I looked up at her sweet face, messy red hair and tear- streaked face, I needed her so fuckin' bad. I wanted my wife, my Eva.

Scooping her tight little ass off the floor, she felt light as a feather. Fuck me for drinking so damn much tonight, getting us to the bedroom in one piece was a miracle, especially since Eva thought taking off her top and bra would speed up the process. I tossed her down on our king-sized bed. Her red hair fell out of its high ponytail. She sprung up and was immediately lifting my shirt overhead. Her greedy little mouth kissed every inch of my chest until she was trailing downward to the promise land. I wobbled at the foot of the bed as Eva undid my buckle and whipped the belt from my jeans. Eyeing my belt, she peeked up at me through those thick lashes.

"No fuckin' games tonight, baby." I took the belt from her hands; Eva had a weak spot for a pink ass. Fuck me, I loved that woman.

Silent, I heard her long nails unclip the button, and take ahold of my thick metal zipper. As I kicked off my boots, Eva slid down my jeans and briefs. Sitting back on her heels, Eva paused with her hands on top of her thighs.

"What's wrong?" I pushed a strand of her hair behind her shoulder.

"I'm just memorizing you, that's all." A sad look crossed her face, and my chest tightened.

"Come here, baby." Trying to not think about the aftermath of tonight, I stroked myself as I stared down at Eva's tits, her perfectly sized breasts and her tiny dusty-pink nipples. They hardened before my eyes.

Leaning back, Eva's legs swung around in front of her and her hair spread out underneath her. Christ, she looked like a fucking angel. Pressing up on her feet, with her shoulders against the bed, her work-out pants and panties were gone in one fell swoop. Seeing her bare legs drift apart made my dick pulse. Her manicured nails drifted down the front of her body.

"Show me how wet you are." I widened my stance to gain my balance while Eva's fingers spread her folds, showing me that pretty pink pussy. That said pussy was gleaming with her arousal. It's all mine.

"I'm soaking wet, Hunter." Her hips rolled up to her hand and she stroked her middle finger up her center and put it to her lips. Eva made sure she had my attention as her tongue slowly circled her fingertip.

"Fuck, baby," I grunted as she went for seconds. Eva dipped two fingers into herself as her left hand massaged her left breast, rolling her outstretched palm over her hard nipples. As she went harder, I pumped faster. I used my left hand to adjust and tug on my balls, delaying getting off. Shit, I was going to ruin her pussy tonight.

"Hunter!" My name rolled off her tongue as she sucked air in-between her teeth. Eva pulled her hand back up, rubbing her wetness on to her right breast, further hardening her nipple. Right as she was about to lick her fingers clean, I reached out and grabbed ahold of her wrist.

"Tsk- tsk, you know better than to hold out on me. My greedy girl, going in for seconds."

"If you don't do something in the next five seconds, I'm finishing the job myself." Fuck me; I knew she was telling the truth because she had done it before. Early in our dating phase, she beat me to the punch and I spanked her ass to the point where she couldn't wear jeans for three straight days. I chuckled to myself at the memory. I lazily slapped her hands away from her pussy. I grabbed her ankles and pulled her ass to the edge of the bed.

The bed stood up on a platform, that when Eva's pussy was hanging over the edge, she was perfectly lined up to my cock to get a proper fucking. I rocked forward onto my tiptoes, dragging my pulsing dick between her folds. Eva moaned as she arched her back off the bed and her hands reached down on either side of her to hold onto my legs. My thighs flexed under her long nails as they grazed across my skin.

I felt her heels press down into my traps, urging me to quit my teasing.

"Hunter," Eva begged. I could never get tired of hearing that. But I needed to suck it all up now while I could before she was gone.

"You're ready for me?"

"Fuck yes, now!" She dug her nails into my thighs. I held onto her ankles and plunged inside her. Eva let out a heavy sigh. Her arms went overhead and gripped the bed sheets. Her tits danced about as I found my rhythm. My balls slapped her round ass, making Eva beg for more. I let go of her ankles and threaded my arms between her feet, wrapping her legs around my waist. I pulled her up off the bed so we could switch spots. I sat on the edge of the bed as Eva straddled my cock. My right arm gripped the nape of her neck and hair. I guided her mouth to mine as my left hand reached around her waist and held her tight to me. One thing Eva excelled at was being on top. I swear she rode my dick like she was riding a damn mechanical bull. Her thick hips rolled and bucked against me. My feet planted firmly on the step of the bed's platform.

"Oh God!" Eva wrapped her arms around my neck as she picked up the speed.

"How does it feel?" I groaned into her ear as I licked her shoulder that was a mix of sweet and salty.

"So damn good, baby, don't stop." Those were the only words of encouragement I needed as I flipped us back around. I laid her down on her side; Eva bent her knees as I positioned myself between her now scissored legs. My left knee came between hers and my right cradled her ass. She grabbed onto the mattress for support as I raised her left leg to rest her ankle in the crook of my neck. That position got me the furthest inside Eva. We fit together like fucking puzzle pieces.

"Fuck," I grunted as I hammered into her. I knew she'd be left with bruises and a sore pussy tomorrow. Eva got off on me being rough with her.

"Harder! Oh yes, right there!" Her hips rocked against mine, and I could feel her insides clench around me. She was almost there. She rode out her orgasm, and collapsed down on the bed, and held on for me to finish. Eva's tightening pussy milked it out of me. My dick pulsed and I filled Eva's pussy to the hilt. Feeling my warmth coat her gave me a sense of dominance, control and pride. I collapsed down on top of her. Our sweaty bodies were out of breath. I rolled onto my back and took Eva with me. I grabbed my shirt off the floor and tossed it to Eva. She placed it between her thighs to capture the overflow of cum. Once we caught our breath, I traced Eva's jawline, and hooked my pointer finger under her chin, and gently tilted her chin upward. Knowing, she tipped her head back to look at me, smile and kiss me. I held her so fucking tight that night. The alcohol and exhaustion caught up with me. Eva's breathing slowed and she snuggled up to my chest. I held onto her naked body as I fell asleep.

The next morning...

I stretched and reached for Eva on her side of the bed. The sheets were cold and empty. I shot upward. On her nightstand laid an envelope that read my name. The closet and dressers were opened, and emptied. The pit in my stomach told me what I already knew. Eva wasn't there. My wife was gone.

present ...

Get the fuck out of here. If Eva thinks I'll fight for her after all this time, she has another thing coming. Just as long as we don't have any further contact, I'm good. Get Nicole and my brothers out of here and go home. Eva has her new Old Man to keep her company. That motherfucker. I thought of his filthy hands all over her body- images of her butt ass naked riding him, and his fingers marking her with his grip. I felt a wave of territorial heat come over me- I was fucking pissed. I'm going to fuckin' kill him just for being with my ex. Well, I guess I can't say ex. He's just fucking my wife. Christ, that sounds fucked up.

Nicole

the next day...

I BARELY SLEPT A WINK LAST NIGHT. I COULDN'T FUCKING STAND THIS PLACE. I just needed to see Jeremy. On cue, Eva came barging into my room, that woman was on a mission. She tossed a black duffle bag down on the foot of my bed.

"What the hell is that?" I sat up and pulled my knees to my chest.

"You look like shit. Get a shower; make sure you're clean-shaven, and dressed. You go on in two hours."

"Go on?"

"Yeah, sweetheart. Or have you already forgotten what Jax told you, 'you needed your rest,' for your performance tonight." She winked at me and headed for the door.

"I can't believe you stand for the shit he does to you," I called out to her as her hand reached for the doorknob. Eva paused and turned to me.

"Sometimes people aren't what they seem, Nicole." *What the fuck was that supposed to mean? Fuckin' riddles.*

After Eva left the room, I unzipped the bag she had left for me. I overturned the duffle and shook out the contents onto my bed. Not much but bits of fabric, makeup, hair styling products, and of course... heels.

Fuck me.

All of the lingerie was Devil's red. It was skimpy, and left little to the imagination. I settled on a crisscross front corset and a strappy cheeky panty. I rolled up my red thigh highs that were embroidered with elaborate dark maroon stitching around the tops. I had just finished drying my hair when Eva waltzed on in. She admired me from head to toe, and looked pleased.

"What?" I questioned her through the mirror on my vanity.

"You just remind me of someone." She looked distant. Eva almost seemed soft. Something changed since the previous day.

"And who would that be? You?" I sneered, as I laid out the make-up in front of me.

"Actually, yes." Eva moved the heating base of the hot rollers closer to her as she picked up the comb sitting on the vanity. "Let me do this for you," she offered as she moved toward me and gestured toward my hair. I shrugged. *Okay, the ice queen may have a soul after all.*

As she started to comb the front of my hair, she said, "You

remind me of me. Not me now, but me before there was a me and Jax." As Eva separated my hair and began to set the rollers it reminded me of when my Mom used to do my hair for special occasions. This got my thoughts rolling from my Mom, my Dad, the drugs, my OD, high school, bonfires, Jeremy and my V-card. Fucked up train of thought but it all led me to thinking about that night. My left hand instinctively cradled my right and I flexed my pink finger, lost in the memory.

CHAPTER 8

Nicole

past ...

"Please, just come out. I'm sure Mason would go." Roxy shook my arm like a rag doll as she begged me with puppy dog eyes.

"I don't know, Rox." I stood to pace the room.

"What don't you know about?" Roxy pushed off my bed, and walked over to me with worried eyes.

"I don't know if I'm ready to face the real world. Mine has been so fucked lately, that I don't know which end is up." I pulled away from her and combed my fingers through my hair.

"Babe, this is your head, a.k.a. up..." she gently placed her palm on my forehead, "and this would be your rockin' ass, a.k.a down." She reached around me and slapped my backside, resulting in a laugh. A simple laugh, who knew how good that would feel?

"Thank you for setting me straight. I thought I lost my way." I swatted her away from me.

"What was that?" Roxy cocked her head to the side.

"What was what?" My eyebrows furrowed.

"Did you just make a joke? Oh thank you, baby Jesus, she's coming back to me!" Roxy threw herself at me.

"Rox!" I giggled as we tumbled back onto my bed. After our laughter subsided, Roxy and I looked at each other while catching our breath.

"Okay, I'll go. I'll text Mason and let him know."

"Good, I'm glad. I'll see you in an hour." Roxy kissed my cheek and left me to get ready for my first night out since the series of events that have wrecked my life. And by series I mean- my father killing my mother for finding out I wasn't his biological daughter, me becoming an addict, putting myself through hell and OD'ing. Just a few things, that's all. I grabbed my phone and texted Mason.

Me: Hey

Mason: Hey, what's up?

Me: Bonfire tonight at 9?

Mason: Sure babe, the lake?

Me: Yeah, Rox and I will meet you there

Mason: K, see you then

I tossed my cell on the bed as I grabbed my bath towel. Mason was alright. He played sports, football, I think. Maybe I should have paid better attention when we went on our first date the other night. Oops.

I dressed in a simple loose gray tee, black leggings and my favorite flats. I didn't do anything special with my hair other than blow-dry it. My makeup was just bronzer and liquid eyeliner to do my infamous cat-eye look, and a muted pink lip-gloss. Believe me, this was the most I have done with myself in a long ass time. It felt good to feel like a girl again. I spritzed on my favorite perfume, gave myself the once-over and headed over to Roxy's place.

I stood on the porch of the Moretti's home. I shot a texted Roxy to let her know I was out front. The rule was: if you were going out for fun, don't ring the doorbell. You didn't have to deal with getting hounded by all the males. Just as I hit send on the message, the front door swung open.

"That was fast-" my sentence was cut off as I looked up and saw who it was. Jeremy, not Roxy. There he stood in his riding boots, black semi-baggy jeans and a fitted white tee under a black zip-up hoodie. Jeremy held onto the doorknob with a scowl on his face. My hair gusted over my shoulders with the breeze from the front door.

"Where are you two headed?" Jeremy fished out his lighter from his front right pocket of his jeans. He plucked the cigarette that was tucked behind his ear, and put it to his lips as he stepped outside. I went to step backwards as he invaded my personal space, but Jeremy's free hand enclosed around my wrist.

"Out." I was irritated; he knew this was my first time out since everything happened. Why the hell did he have to treat me like a fucking child?

"Out, where?" The red ember glowed as he inhaled his first drag. The smoke clouded around us.

"And you care?"

"Fuck yes, anything that concerns my sister, then yes- it's my business to know."

"Okay, papa bear." I over exaggerated my eye roll.

"Roll them eyes again, and they're going to get stuck in the back of your head, little girl." Jeremy's deep voice vibrated off my chest.

"Last time I checked, Roxy already has a father to look after her." I crossed my arms.

"What about you?" Jeremy tipped his chin towards me.

"What do you mean, 'what about me'?"

"Who's watching out for you?"

"Myself." I was getting defensive, and he knew it.

"Wrong."

"Wrong?"

"You have your MC. Moretti, Rox, Chase...me."

"You, huh?" My eyebrow cocked up in surprise.

"Yeah, feels like I'm a little responsible for you now that I've brought you back to life." His thick eyebrows wiggled.

"Ugh, spare me, Jer. Don't think you can hold that over my head my entire life."

"Spare you? You're so damn ungrateful sometimes, Nic."Jeremy threw his cigarette butt down between us, causing me to jump back so it didn't land on the top of my foot.

"Watch it!" I yelled at him as my phone chirped with a text message. His eyes shot down to my phone.

"Who's that?"

"Mason." I swear Jeremy's eyes went dark right in front of me.

"That pussy," he growled. Yes, literally growled at me.

"Do you have to refer to any guy I date as a pussy? I don't date pussies, makes me sounds like a lesbian, and to be quite honest, I'm strictly dickly. You need to broaden your vocabulary, biker boy." I played with the hem of my t-shirt. Jeremy's eyes quickly glanced at my hands and back up to my face with a knowing smirk. Playing with the edges of soft fabrics was a self-soothing thing I did and he knew it.

Jeremy let out a deep belly chuckle; it was rare that I heard that laugh, but when I did, it did things to my insides- good things.

"What?" I dropped my hands as he took a step closer to me, our chests touching. The heat of his body permeated me as the thin fabric between us almost seemed nonexistent.

"I just find it funny, you referring to dick, when you haven't even had any."

"Fuck you!"

"Well, let's go then." Jeremy's arms gripped my hips, slamming mine into his. My hands shot out to his arms as I nearly stumbled forward into him. I acted like I didn't feel the bulge in his jeans that was currently pressing into my hip.

"You're impossible."

"You love it."

"Jer-" My voice faded as he leaned his face down to mine. He knew exactly what he was doing, and the effect that he had on me. I closed my eyes as I felt his warm breath on my face. His nose nuzzled my neck, my ear, then my cheek. I didn't realize I had been holding my breath, until Jeremy told me to breath.

The deep breath I inhaled through my nostrils filled with the scent of his cigarette, leather, and cologne.

"You smell good enough to eat," Jeremy muttered. His eyebrows cocked up and inward.

"Well, if Mason plays his cards right, he'll get to find out." I was lying through my teeth. Jeremy's grip on my hips and ass grounded deeper. Was that a nerve I hit?

"He fuckin' touches you, he's dead." He roughly cupped my face.

"I am dating him, Jer. That kind of gives him the right to, wouldn't it?" My eyes searched his. 'Then you fucking claim me, you bastard!' was what I wanted to shout in his face.

We could hear Roxy inside the house, running down the staircase, shouting back to their father that she was heading out. Jeremy quickly darted his tongue over my bottom lip, his lips covered mine. Just as I was about to further the kiss, the front door flung open.

"Uhh..." Roxy stood there like a deer in headlights.

"I was just telling Nic to call if you girls need anything."

"I'm sure you were. Were you also trying to give her CPR, standing up? You creeper, step away from my friend." Roxy grabbed my hand and hurriedly took us to my car.

Once we arrived at the bonfire, I was sure to avoid the subject with Roxy about Jeremy and what happened on the porch. Hell, I wasn't even sure what the fuck happened. Mason was already sitting by the bonfire that sat along the edge of the lake. Lake Pend Oreille was a big hangout spot for high school students. Spotting Roxy and I, Mason stood up to greet us, giving me a quick hug. I could already smell the beer on his breath. This was going to be a fun night.

After an hour and a couple beers down, everyone was relaxed and having a good time. The buddies that Mason was hanging with for the night seemed to not know their limit. Silly boys, they don't even know what "getting messed up" really is. Roxy and I talked about graduation and what would happen next. I know she's excited to go to college but I also know it's a sore point for her to be leaving Chase, Jeremy's best friend.

"Hey babe," Mason cut into our conversation.

"Yeah?" I sounded faintly annoyed by his drunken slur.

"Let's take a walk down by the water."

"Sure." I looked over at Roxy, and nodded. She took my empty beer bottle and nudged me up off my seat.

We headed down to where the water was lapping at the pebbly beach. Mason was an attractive guy. He stood about 6'0" with shaggy brown hair and hazel eyes. He has a leaner built compared to Jeremy and Chase. I'm always comparing guys to Jeremy, that fucker. Mason had strong features and sweet personality.

"You having fun?" he asked me as he laced our hands together while walking side by side.

"Sure."

"Sure? That doesn't sound promising."

"I just have a lot on my mind." Jeremy.

"Oh yeah? Am I on there?" Mason came to a halt and turned me to face him.

"Maybe." I didn't want to let him down, but he definitely caught wind.

"Maybe, huh? Maybe I can change that to, 'you're all I'm thinking about, Mason'." He bit his lower lip, something that probably should have stirred up some butterflies but my crotch felt zero zing.

"Mason?" I was about to ask him if he wanted to head back, but he cut me off when he dipped his head down to kiss me. Half on and half off my mouth- I wasn't really feeling it. I slowly pulled back, licking my bottom lip. Mason misread my action as me wanting more. He cupped my face and re-connected our mouths. Before I could protest, he licked my lips. I put my palms on his shoulders and pushed.

"Mason, I'm sorry, I can't-"

"Yes, you can. You taste so fucking good, Nicole." One of his hands slipped up under my shirt and over my bra cup.

"I said no!" I was getting pissed.

"That's not what your body is saying." His thumb flicked my nipple, and his hips pushed into mine. His arousal was obvious and unwanted.

"Yeah, 'cause it's fucking cold out here, you fucking asshole." I ripped his arm out from under my shirt, and started walking away from him.

"Nicole!" Mason ran after me.

"Fuck you, Mason."

"Fuck me? Fuck you!" He grabbed my upper arm. I pulled away from him, causing the thin fabric of my shirt to rip. I shrieked as I stumbled backwards, tripping over a large stone. Mason took advantage of my position, forcing himself between my legs.

"Get off me!" I screamed out, praying someone could hear me. Kissing me roughly, Mason dug his fingertips into my hips as he went to pull down my leggings.

"Get the fuck off of her!" I heard Roxy's voice swiftly approaching us. Mason shot his head upward, and I took advantage by winding back and punching him right on the bridge of his nose. I cried out in pain as he rolled to my side and cupped his face. Roxy kicked him right in the ribs.

"You fucker!" she yelled at him as he rolled onto his back groaning in pain.

"You fucking bitch!" he spat out. Roxy grabbed my uninjured hand and pulled me off the beach.

"Let's just get the fuck out of here." My adrenaline was wearing off, my hand throbbed and the tears flowed. I shouldn't have been upset but fuck it- I was. Roxy walked us back to the fire, calling someone along the way. Minutes later a bike was rumbling down to the waterfront.

"You called your bother?!" I groaned as I took the hem of my shirt and wiped under each eye.

"No one fucks with us and gets away with that shit, Nicole. Plus, who else was I going to call?"

Well, not only Jeremy rolled up, but both of our knights on their shiny armor arrived. Chase and Jeremy both kicked their stands out and quickly walked to us. Jeremy's eyes scanned my face as he took off his riding gloves. His eyes stopped at my shoulder, where my shirt was torn and my bra strap was hanging on by a thread. I held my aching hand as I lowered my gaze in embarrassment.

"The party is over, everyone go home!" Jeremy yelled, and everyone was out like a bat out of hell. Mason started to make his way past Jeremy, but Jeremy splayed his fingers on Mason's chest to stop him. A smile crossed Jeremy's face as he put two and two together, my injured hand with Mason's bloody nose. Moving me behind him, Jeremy slowly walked back to Mason.

"You're mine, you mother fucker." Jeremy shoved Mason backwards.

"What the fuck?" Mason yelled out, going chest to chest with Jeremy. Roxy and I backed up to boys' bikes; the warmth of the fire had long left me.

"You like forcing yourself onto girls? Touching them when they don't want to be touched? You get off on it?" Jeremy shoved Mason hard with each question.

"Yeah, when she's offering it up!"

"The fuck I was!" I yelled out, walking back to the two of them, but Jeremy's pinning look made me stop in my tracks. Roxy grabbed my elbow and pulled me back to where she stood with Chase. This was something he was going to take care of. Before I knew it, Jeremy's fist collided with Mason's cheek. My hand shot to my mouth as the two scuffled on the ground. Jeremy was kicking his ass! As Mason tried to crawl away, Jeremy glimpsed to the fire beside him. Grabbing a log that wasn't fully engulfed in the flames, Jeremy gripped Mason by his jeans and belt, and sat on top of him, with his boots on either side of Mason's back

"If you ever think, look, touch, or talk to Nicole again, I'll fucking kill you," Jeremy yelled into Mason's ear as he pressed the hot ember end of the wood onto the back of Mason's hand. I sucked in a sharp breath with my uninjured hand over my mouth and Roxy turned her face into Chase's chest. The stench of burnt flesh filled the air. Mason's screams subsided when Jeremy let up, and he passed out from the pain. That fucker deserved it.

"Take Roxy home, would you, Chase? I'll take it from here." I was frozen in place, staring at the blood stained dirt beside Mason.

After Roxy and Chase headed out, Jeremy focused on me. Gingerly, he reached down to my closed fist.

"It's dislocated," he stated as he inspected my fingers.

"I'd rather that than something else..." I trailed off. I knew he knew the double meaning to that. I didn't let that fucker take my virginity. Jeremy let out a long relieved breath. Seeing him affected, created warmth that pooled in my belly. I stepped closer to him. In a quick jerk, Jeremy pulled my pinky finger straight. I cried out as hot tears pricked my eyes, and pulled my hand back and cradled it to my chest.

"Thank you," I managed to get out.

"Anytime." He tucked a loose strand of hair behind my ear.

"Not just for tonight, but for everything, for saving me, Jer. I wouldn't be here if it weren't for you." I lowered my hands, along with the wall I built so high around myself. Leaning in closer to him, my breaths weren't shallow anymore. They were heavy pants and he took notice.

This was the first time I had said anything about the night Jeremy found me when I overdosed. Sensing my need to be touched, Jeremy cupped my face right before his lips grazed mine. I popped up onto my tiptoes and eagerly kissed him back. I guess I took Jeremy by surprise as he gripped my hair and pulled back from me, both of us gasping for air.

"Nic, if you don't stop, I sure as fuck won't be able to."

"I don't want you to stop, ever."

CHAPTER 9

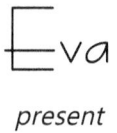va

present

AFTER I SET NICOLE'S HAIR, I HAD TO GET OUT OF THERE BEFORE I DID something stupid, like bond with the girl or some shit. I was starting to lose face. I made my way back to Jax's room. He was in the shower. I heeled off my shoes and stripped out of my clothing. I made my way across our room to the master bathroom. The bathroom best described Jax, masculine and dark. The walls were painted charcoal gray, glossy speckled-black granite countertops with a thickly framed mirror over the sink vanity. The highlight of the room- the huge frameless glass shower with dual showerheads. My eyes studied the fogging glass as his broad back, firm ass, and muscular legs were on display to me. His big hands splayed on the tiled wall. They were held up upright above his head under the streaming water, his shoulders flexed as his right hand slicked back his dark blonde hair. I had to give it to Jax, as dark and fucked up as he was, he was fucking hot.

Feeling my body react to him didn't make me feel guilty anymore. It took a long time for me to "get over" Hunter, and when I met Jax, he filled a void for me. He took me in and made me his, and has done some pretty respectful things. One of which stands out in my mind. If Hunter knew, he would nark me out, or kill me. But if Jax ever found out, he'd undoubtedly kill me too. Fuck. I pushed my thoughts to the back of my mind as I opened the glass door, and the cool air hitting Jax's back caused his head to turn somewhat to the side.

Pushing off the tiled wall, his forearms flexed as he turned towards me, and his arms rose to push back his hair. As much evil that's consumed Jax, he still feels the need to wash away his sins. Jax's blue eyes bore into mine as I made my way closer to him. His thick fingers roughly gripped the side of my hips. The spraying water beaded on my skin. The hot water rolled down my neck, over my breasts, and downward to the rest of my body. My hands wound around his neck. Jax wasn't as big and built as Hunter, but his heavily inked arms and chest were sexy as hell. My weakness. The black and gray intricate portraits, graphics, names and bible verses were beautiful and in a way reminded me of Hunter. I knew that I had Jax as a stand in, maybe that's what helped me do my job. God, that sounds so fucked up.

"Jax?" I whispered as our bodies met. My long fingernails combed the hair at the nape of his neck.

"Yeah, babe?" He pressed his growing erection against me.

"I want you."

"Well, isn't that obvious since you're standing?" *What a dick.*

"Shut the hell up, and just fuck me already, would you?" I cocked my eyebrow up at him in challenge. He gave me the sexiest smirk as he sat down on the tiled bench in the shower, and pulled me on top of his lap. His large palms spread my cheeks apart and he used the tips of his index fingers to guide his cock inside me. Jax took away the pain that I buried deep within myself: burdens, regrets, sorrows and lies. I wish he could fuck it out of me, I really do. But, no matter how hard I try to forget Hunter, it all comes crashing down on me. I bit down on Jax's shoulder as he slid his hands up my back and cupped my shoulders and pulled me downward as his hips thrust up. He filled me up to the hilt. Our face-to-face position put pressure on my most responsive area. My sensitive nipples rubbed against his chest. When I closed my eyelids, all I saw were Hunter's dark eyes. My body recalled how good it felt to have him on top of me again. The way my body was fucking Jax, was exactly what I wanted to be doing to Hunter right now. Shit, I'm fucking ruined.

Jax moved my wet hair over my right shoulder and his eyes had sought mine. He looked at me like he was looking for forgiveness for all of his sins. But no, Jax Solomon was a monster. As much as I loathed him, part of me had also grown to love him. Parts of me went numb and others went dark when I got myself involved with the Knights MC. Four years have gone by. Four years of harboring my secret from Hunter. Three years of keeping my life hidden from Jax. Two days of denying my re-kindled feelings for Hunter. And only one person that I needed to protect, my own flesh and blood.

past ...

Today was Valentine's Day, a.k.a. Victoria's Secret night and I had just arrived for my shift at Bottom's Up. Lingerie, babydolls, corsets, and garters flooded the dressing room. We were all getting dressed to impress. Bending over toward my mirror, I pushed the girls up and together. Making sure they were nearly spilling out of my gray and black lace corset. I tightened the ribbon bows on my garter belt.

"Damn honey, you going to make those men trip over their dicks tonight." Reese giggled as she adjusted the plunging neckline of her red lace halter babydoll.

"Me? What about you?" I slapped her ass.

"Yeah, yeah. I don't mess with the guests." She applied a flat red lip stain to her lips.

"Rule to live by?"

53

"For me at least. I had to learn my lesson the hard way." She left me to finish my makeup.

Hmm, I'll have to ask Reese about that one later. Tonight was packed. The drinks flowed as the girls were making it rain tonight. The more liquored up the visitors were, the more gratitude they left for tips.

"Goddamn! If that isn't the most perfect ass I've ever seen in my life." And if this isn't the most repulsive man I've ever seen in my life. Mr. Grabby-Ass has been on my shit all fucking night.

"Another round?" I asked the other men sitting with the asshole.

"Yeah, another round, and a round of that sweet piece of ass of yours." I felt a hand roughly grasp the back of my thigh and start to travel upward. Right as I slammed down my serving tray, that hand stopped its upward journey. I rapidly turned around to see some biker boy gripping Mr. Grabby- Ass's wrist. He brought him to his knees.

"Keep your fuckin' filthy hands to yourself!" Biker boy practically growled at him.

"Maybe if she didn't put it out there for the world to see, this is a fucking strip club, isn't it?"

"This place is strictly hands off, asshole."

"She didn't mind it, did you, sweetheart?" He puckered his lips at me as I sneered down at him. Biker boy gripped the man's mouth and threw his ass backwards into the booth.

"I can handle myself." I shoved biker boy aside and made my way back to the bar.

I could feel his eyes burning into my backside.

"Shit, Eva. You know, no girl has ever talked to Hunter that way." Hunter. Yes, I knew his name, even though I shouldn't. I've studied his handsome face, and have researched him. I knew Hunter Sabatino like the back of my hand. He was my target, and it was just my dumb ass fault for crushin' on him as well. I shrugged off Reese's comment.

"Well, maybe he should let women handle their own problems, instead of trying to be the man in shining armor, or in his case, the man on shining armor. Not every girl needs rescuing." I watched as

Reese popped the caps off three beers and placed them on my tray.

"Well, fuckin' excuse me if I felt that not every girl should be felt up like that." His warm voice caressed my ear and neck, his arms caged me against the bar top, but he leaned back far enough to not touch my body. I tried to ignore my body's initial reaction to his presence. The smell of his cologne and leather permeated the air around me.

"Like I said before, I can handle myself." Roughly, I reared my hips and ass back into his groin. What I thought was going to knock the wind out of him, only resulted in the opposite. His right hand sought my hipbone and pulled me back into him and a grunt rumbled his broad chest.

"I bet you can, baby." Hunter chuckled into my ear and goose bumps broke out over my skin.

"I have work to get back to, *baby*." I emphasized his childish nickname, secretly loving the shit out of it.

"Well then, don't let me keep you." Hunter gently pushed me forward as he stepped back, and caressed my backside before he walked to his booth full of Hell's Rebels members.

"Goodness, woman. I about need a cigarette after watching you two. Please don't remind me of all the sex I'm not having." Reese did a quick catcall before a customer was waving her down for another refill.

"Yeah, yeah." I shook my head at her and delivered my order of drinks.

For the next hour of my shift I could feel his warm eyes on me. I'm pretty sure my panties could dissolve right off my body. I felt butterflies swarm my belly and my demand to get laid was rising. I had to set a private room for Ruby to perform. Last but not least, the champagne in an ice bucket with rose petals. Someone had it bad for her to request this setup. It was our top Valentine's Day package, which equaled beaucoup bucks. Just as I straightened my back after sprinkling the rose petals, the door to the room opened. The dark hallway lighting didn't let me see his face.

"Just a minute, and she will be in." I threw the stems in the trashcan.

He didn't say a word, still standing there.

"You can sit, you know? Can I get you a drink, sir?" I gave him my full attention.

Before I knew what was happening in the small room, the man took two steps towards me, covering his mouth with mine. I was caught off guard, and ready to plan my attack- but then it hit me. That smell. Leather and spice. Hunter. My struggle against him came to a halt. His hands wrapped around my waist, and gripped my ass cheeks in each hand. I let out a small squeal, and he took the advantage and took my bottom lip into his mouth. The taste of bourbon hit my tongue as he sucked and nipped on my bottom lip as I did the same to his upper lip. My tall heels allowed me to reach up his strong arms and drive straight into his hair with my hands. As Hunter groaned, I moaned. He guided me backwards to the round cushioned ottoman shaped stage, where Ruby was going to perform.

His large frame bent over mine, and my knees fell apart as he settled in between my legs. Hunter pulled down the front of my corset and latched onto my breast. The tight boning of the lingerie forced whatever tits I had up and inward, right in Hunter's face. My body bowed upwards to his, and my hands that were in his hair forced his mouth further into my cleavage. His mouth vacuumed all of the air out, and sucked my full nipple into his mouth, and his hand palmed my other breast. His outstretched palm rolled my already taught bud. Hunter's skillful hands prepped me before he made his switch. The cool air hit my wet nipple, made me suck in a sharp breath. I felt his erection through his jeans; the thick zipper of his jeans pressed into my thigh.

"Fuck," I hissed as Hunter bit down on my breast. What was up with him and biting? Whatever it was, I fucking loved it.

"I knew you'd like it rough."

"Just shut up and keep going," I moaned. He stood up, and his pointer finger trailed down the body of my corset and followed the edge of my panties. Obviously he felt their dampness by now, and if the lights were on in here, he'd see my blush.

"Goddamn," he groaned as he pushed the thin material aside, and his fingers dipped into my wetness. I felt the palm of his hand grind against my already throbbing clit. I circled my hips upward; making Hunter's hand hit all the right places. Just as I was riding his hand to reach my climax, his fingers left me in an instant. My eyes shot open, Hunter's face was lit by the blue mood lighting. That sexy ass smirk splayed on his lips as he looked down at me.

"Why did you stop?" I grabbed at his shirt and yanked him down to me.

" Just wanted to see you all wanton on my fingers."

"I wasn't done yet." I guided his hands back down to my panties. This time, I pulled my panties aside, and brought his fingers to my center. I heard Hunter suck his teeth before taking over again. I came hard and fast. I can't remember the last time I was finger-blasted into oblivion, but Goddamn, that shit made me see stars.

"Well, now that we've been properly introduced, my name is Hunter."

"Well, then I'd say that is one hell of a handshake you have there." I propped myself up on my elbows and watched Hunter adjust himself in his jeans. He tucked his erection up under the waistband of his jeans. Now, I was the one to smirk.

"Well, you let me know when you want to get reacquainted." He leaned down over me and kissed my cheek. I breathed him in as my eyelids drifted closed. I was stunned, horny, and actually impressed.

"I will," I whispered into his ear. Hunter stood again and left me there to bask in the aftereffects of my climax.

CHAPTER 10

JEREMY
present

THE FUCKING KINK IN MY NECK WAS KILLING ME. I HAD MY OWN HOLDING CELL, IF you want to call it that. It was just a room with a stained concrete floor, stale air, and a bucket to piss in. It's just my lucky fucking day. I couldn't remember the last time I ate, but I was fucking starving. I didn't want to sleep, but I kept nodding off. I sat in the corner of the room, with my head leaned against the wall. I zeroed in on a hole in the wall that was flawlessly round. Abruptly the door to my room opened, causing it to slam against the wall behind it and leaving a dent in the dry wall. I guess that's where that hole came from, no one knew how to fucking open a door properly.

"Get up," Hunter's wifey yelled at me.

"The fuck?" I refused her.

"I said up, now. Let's fucking go." She popped her hands on her hourglass shaped hips.

My eyes scanned her pin-up figure body. Her red hair wasn't my preferred color, but it fit her. She had huge tits, a tiny waist that was already painted with a tight-ass sheer tank with a black bra underneath. Those thick hips were encased in tight black leather leggings and some fucking hot stiletto heels. I'll give it to Hunter, his wife was fucking hot.

"What are you smiling at? Let's go, Romeo."

"I'm smiling at the fact that Hunter has a wife."

"And what would be so funny about that, huh?" She tapped the toe of her heel on the floor as her hair swung back over her shoulder.

"When he was after my girl, he was married. Fuckin' figures." I saw her eyes flash with hurt for a second before she quickly regained her composure.

"Speaking of your girl, Jax has a surprise for you." I walked towards the doorway, and then abruptly came to a halt, causing Eva to crash into my back. She sucked her teeth in frustration.

"If you don't mind me asking, what happened with you two?"

"Yes, I do mind you asking. Some stories are better left unsaid, now move." She shoved me through the doorway.

Interesting.

Eva led me back to the clubhouse, the main dance area where I saw Nicole performing a mere two days ago. It was packed wall to wall with cuts. The liquor flowed, mirrors full of coke were being passed around, and naked women flocked the floor. Eva sat me in a booth along with Hunter and Derrick. She left us guarded by two big fuckers with their occupied gun holsters, ready to throw down.

I nodded over to the guys.

"The fuck is going on?" Derrick whispered as we all leaned on the table.

"The fuck if I know." Hunter put his cuffed wrists onto the table to join ours. Isn't this just fucking cute?

"Someone should be coming for us soon." I looked straight ahead to keep a look out.

"Well, how soon is soon? Shit, we've been here for what, two days? I'm going fucking crazy sitting in that room." Derrick sounded anxious and stressed. A windowless room probably wasn't the best situation for a guy who has PTSD.

"Relax, D." I leveled my hand and motioned it down, parallel to the table top.

"Jax talk to you at all? You see Nicole?" Hunter sounded anxious as his eyes scanned the room.

"Yeah, he "talked" to me alright. That mother fucker." I recalled the vision of Nicole on her knees before him. My teeth clenched.

"Nicole?" Derrick asked with an intense look in his eye.

My eyes peered at Derrick. I was still pissed at him for giving her E at the club that one night. But I had a fucking right. He had fucked with her in the past. I'm pretty sure some shit went down between them, and I didn't fucking like it. But I got him in this mess, and I'm a man of my word so I will get him out.

"I'll worry about Nicole. I saw her and she was fine. I want to know what the fuck we are doing out here. I don't fucking like it." I laced my fingers together, and then the spotlights illuminated the stage. There were a flock of girls filing out onto the stage in a single file line, holding large feathered fans that nearly covered their entire bodies. Doing a synchronized dance, they revealed themselves; each wore a different styled panty. Thong, briefs, bikini, shorts, G-string, you name it- they wore it. After their little show and dance, they all huddled together with their clustered fans fluttering as the lights dimmed down. The spotlight above projected down on what they were about to reveal. All at once the girls moved away, exposing Nicole.

The breath that I was holding in my lungs left me. Fuckin'-A, she was beautiful. Realization hit me that every pair of eyes in this place was on my Old Lady, and she was wearing close to nothing. My jaw clenched along with my fists. She stood sideways with her hip popped. My eyes trailed up her lean legs, pausing at where her garter belt connected to the top of her stockings. Her smooth skin shimmered under the lights. Her hair and makeup were done perfectly, but her eyes were scanning the room in a panic. Then they found me and I saw the fear in them.

The music started and Nic closed her eyes as she took a deep breath. Jax was doing just what he said he was going to do. Make her the club's entertainment, and his own. Warrant's "Cherry Pie" flooded through the clubhouse. Fucking typical, and fucking convenient that Nicole was sporting those cherry red colors.

"Easy." Hunter leaned over to me. He noticed I was starting to stand up in the booth. Remembering where I was, I sat back down. I did all that I could do, which was to watch Nicole perform. She was stiff and hesitant at first. I saw her look to the side of the stage, directly at Jax who stood with his arms crossed and a shit-eating grin on his smug face. The men of the Devil's MC were hooting and hollering for her to give them what they wanted, a show. Her round hips rolled, and their catcalls were almost deafening. They all wanted her, over my goddamn dead body. Each one of those fuckers was going to die. Nicole stared straight at Jax as her demeanor switched gears- she was going to give him what he wanted. I bit down on my clenched fist that I had resting at my mouth.

A single steel chair was placed on stage. Nicole grabbed ahold of the back of the chair, and the entire room caught sight of her gorgeous ass. A heavily tattooed man leaned up on stage and slapped her ass. Swiftly she spun on her heel with her hand raised, but Jax caught her attention. She looked back down at the man who had just placed his fuckin' hands on her, placed her heel on his shoulder and seductively but roughly pushed him back down to his seat. I wish that heel went right through that cunt licker's flesh. Going for the chair again, she spun the back of the chair to face the crowd. Biting her lip, she straddled the seat. Christ. Nicole was wearing crotchless panties. Her pussy was on display for each and every single set of eyes in here. The room erupted in a satisfied roar. Nic's eyes were on me, pleading for me to stay calm. But that wasn't fucking happening. Derrick and Hunter each placed a cuffed hand on my shoulder as I stood, knocking the table out from the booth. The fuck I was going to sit through this shit.

Jax followed Nicole's line of vision and his face broke out into a smile. This is what he wanted. Stepping out on the stage, Nicole stood up from the chair and stepped away from him. Jax grabbed the back of the chair, spun it around and sat down. He patted his goddamn lap. Nicole froze. Halfway getting out of the seat, he grabbed her waist and his club brothers went fucking crazy. His left hand splayed across her stomach as she stood between his legs, facing forward. Her head dropped for a brief second. I could see his lips moving, mouthing, "dance" to her as his right hand slapped her ass. Nicole's jaw clenched and she slowly started her routine back up. She placed her hands on the tops of his thighs; dropped her ass, and then brought it back up, pressed into Jax's crotch.

"I'm going to fuckin' kill him!" I charged the tabletop again, knocking it over this time. The two men guarding our table pulled their pieces on me. The barrels of their guns pointed to either side of my temples. The music cut in the club and Nicole froze, demanding Jax to tell his men to back down.

"It looks like Moretti wants a better view, bring him closer!" Jax yelled out.

"You heard him." They grabbed me by the crook of my elbows and dragged me up to the stage. Front and center. Derrick and Hunter joined me as well. Great, let's all get a close up of this fucked up situation. Jax snapped his fingers to cue the music. Nicole was stiff as a board, until Jax grabbed her around the waist again, and pulled her to his front.

I WANTED TO CRAWL UNDER A ROCK AND DIE. JAX WAS HUMILIATING ME, AND killing Jeremy at the same time. Now my lady business is on display for this whole damn club. I could feel the blush of my embarrassment spread across my chest and face. Thank God, the spotlights on the ceiling rafters drowned everyone in the crowd out. My eyes squinted as I felt the sweat bead down my neck and between my breasts. I felt Jax's arm snake around my waist, and he pulled me backwards toward him. The exposed flesh on my ass felt the warmth of his chest through the exposed part of his thin shirt from underneath his cut. His fingertips glided up along the sides of my thighs. I could feel his calloused hands over the hosiery on my legs. It made me shudder when I felt him flick my garter belt, and it snap up against my thigh as he unfastened my front right hose. Moving further up, I held my breath, knowing where his destination was. As Jax's fingertips trailed up to my pussy, he paused. I peeked down to see his hands weren't even on me anymore, and Jax had a sickened expression on his face. *What the fuck?*

"You!" Jax yelled, pushing me away as he stood, and pointed to my guys. They all looked just as confused as I was.

"Fucking cut the music and put the fucking lights on!" Jax roared, and before he even finished his sentence, his wishes were granted.

"Who the fuck are you?" Jax yelled as he put one hand on the stage, hopped down onto the main floor and got right in Hunter's face. Hunter's instincts kicked in and he bumped his chest against Jax's and shoved him away.

"Stop it!" I pleaded.

Jeremy and Derrick were there to back Hunter up.

"Don't worry about who the fuck I am," Hunter spat at him.

What in God's name was this about?

"I want him in my office now," Jax commanded, and just like that, Hunter was plucked from the crowd and was gone. Jeremy looked up at me, and I started to go to him. Fuck this shit. He made it to the edge of the stage as I knelt down. My fingertips skimmed the stubble on his cheek before my hand was suddenly snatched away by Jax.

"And what the fuck do you think you're doing?" The rage in his eyes was something I hadn't seen before, and it scared the shit out of me.

"Just let them go!"

"No!" Jeremy snarled as Jax basically palmed my lower face and shoved me backwards to fall onto my ass. My knees squeezed together as I tried to cover my out and about lady business, but Jax grabbed both of my wrists, hauled me up and over to one of his men.

"Put her away. I need to take care of some business." Jax

motioned me away and his attention focused on Hunter. The last glimpse I had before I was dragged off the stage was Jeremy and Derrick going face to face with Devil's MC members.

CHAPTER 11

HUNTER

"WAIT HERE." AN MC MEMBER PRESSED ME DOWN INTO A SEAT IN FRONT OF A large wooden table. This room was where the Devil's MC held Church. Jax had some serious balls taking me here. What the fuck did he want with me? Just as I finished my train of thought, the main doors opened and Jax entered with a manila envelope in hand.

"The fuck do you want?" I rolled my shoulder back, and cocked my head back. It was the basic alpha male stance. Motherfucker wants to go? Then let's fucking go.

"Shut the fuck up." Jax slammed the door shut and took his seat at the head of the table. The only lighting in the room were spotlights on the table. Jax sat in the fading darkness.

"Mother fucker, you brought me here. What the fuck for?" I clenched my fists on the table in front of me. My veins grew thicker every time my hands opened and closed. Without a word, he opened the folder that was sitting in front of him. He tossed an 8x10 photograph of Eva in front of me. I stopped the sliding picture and spun it to face me. There was her beautiful face staring right back at me. The photograph was in black and white. She sat in front of a café drinking coffee and reading on her tablet. She looked innocent, happy even. The only thing I didn't like about the photograph was that she had no idea she was being watched.

"How do you know her?"

"I don't." I turned the photograph back around and slid it back towards him.

"Maybe you didn't get a good look." Jax palmed the picture and put it back in my face, "I'll ask again, how the fuck to do you know Eva?"

"I said-" Jax cut me off.

"Stop fucking lying!" he shouted.

"She's your old lady, shouldn't you be asking her?"

"Oh I plan on it." His dirty smirk made my stomach turn.

"What's your beef with me? You have no concern when it comes to me."

"My family is my concern."

"And what does that have to do with me? Sounds like a personal problem. Like I said, talk to your woman." Those words tasted like shit.

Jax re-opened the folder on the tabletop. He picked up a smaller-sized photograph.

"You don't want to know how I know you're lying?" He angled his eyebrow.

"I'm good." I rolled my seat backwards and stood up. Just as I was about to beat my fist on the door, I heard the picture flick over towards my end of the table. It was eating at me to see the picture. Peering over my shoulder, I saw the picture lying face down. I rotated my body toward the table, and plucked the picture up.

"You take a look at that picture and then re-think your answer to my earlier question." Jax talked with a Black & Mild cigar hanging on his lips. The spark from his lighter lit his face.

My eyes scanned the picture in my hand. My heart stopped. This has got to be a fucking joke. I placed the picture back on the table and pounded on the door. Devils greeted me and took me back to my holding room. I tried to process what I had just seen. I couldn't wait for Eva's next visit; she had a lot of explaining to do.

CHASE

I PULLED UP TO OUR HOUSE AND WENT INSIDE KNOWING THAT ROXY JUST PUT baby Gio to bed.

"Babe?" I called out to her. I tossed my keys onto the coffee table and toed off my riding boots.

"Yeah?" She walked into the front room wearing a short black cotton robe while she braided her long hair. Roxy paused and gave me a quick kiss. I rewarded her with a swat on the ass.

"You hear from Nic at all?"

"Mmm, no I haven't, why? What did Jeremy do now?" That made me laugh.

"Nothing that I know of, yet. Nicole, Jer, and Hunter are M.I.A."

"Maybe they're busy in a ménage a trios," Rox snickered as she pushed the front of her body to mine. Her arms came around my neck, and a small sigh escaped her lips. I enjoyed being able to wrap myself around her. Before, her expanding belly stood in my way.

"Nice, babe. It's been too quiet at the clubhouse. After church, the three of them seemed to up and disappear. Cell phones are off. Thinking we should be starting to worry." Roxy's small hands drifted down my shoulders and found their way under my cut. She ran her fingertips over my chest. She knew exactly what she was doing.

I inhaled her sweet scent. "Rox," I groaned as I palmed her ass.

"Mmm hmm?" Her innocent eyes fluttered open as she bit down on her bottom lip.

"You make it hard to focus, you know that?" I exhaled out through my nostrils.

"Because you have this between your legs?" Rox wrapped her hand around my hardening dick. *Goddamn, I love this woman.*

"Fuck." I gripped the back of her neck and slammed my mouth down on hers. Someone needs to teach her a lesson on not making someone lose his train of thought.

"Fuck me now, Chase!" Roxy groaned into my open mouth. *Christ!*

I gripped her thick braid, twisted it into my fist and pulled back. Rox's chin rose as a gasp fell from her lips, music to my fucking ears.

"We will worry about them later," I grumbled and whisked her off to bed.

the next morning...

"Moretti, I think we need to move fast. No one has heard from either of them. And Roxy hasn't heard anything from Nicole. Which is fucking uncommon- so something is up." I rested my forearms against the large oak table.

"Where were the boys last? We need to piece together a timeline."

"The last place was when we held church the other night. We were planning how we were going to get Nic." I trailed off as I just realized what I said.

"Fuck." Moretti let out a groan.

"Shit, you think he went for her by himself?" All the members around the table honed in on the conversation.

"Yeah, I think he went for her, but not alone. My son is smarter than that. Unfortunately, he's fucking dumb enough to go without his club. If he's alive when we get there, I'm killing him." Moretti slammed his fist down, the vibrations made their way to my now clenched fist.

"Let's get eyes up there. We ride out tonight, see what shit storm we are about to get in." I ordered two of our best Prospects, Wyatt and Eli, to take the ride up to Sand Point. The boys nodded, accepting their ride out.

"We will see what the report is when the boys get up there." The small wooden hammer slammed down on the block and Moretti dismissed church. I kicked back my seat quickly, and hiked up my lowered jeans. It was just Moretti and I left in the room.

"Chase?"

"Yeah, Prez?" I smoothed my hand over the short beard I was growing out.

"I know you understand how important this is to me. This is my blood. This is my family, and your family too. I know I was hard on you all those years, but you know I was doing it to protect my baby girl. I don't need to say how much I fucking love my kids, because you already know. Chase, you're like another son to me. Since your father passed, I promised him I would keep you alive, and that you'd always be in our family. Not just the MC family. You do a damn good job, son. Make me fuckin' proud and get Jeremy out alive so that he can finally make a honest man of himself." He slapped his hand over my shoulder.

"Prez-" I tried to cut in. Fucking hearing about my Pops brought up too many fucking emotions.

"How is my daughter?"

"As good as she can be."

"Good, now keep it that way. We will talk when we hear from the Prospects."

"Got it." I headed outside for my bike and rode home to see my woman. Keeping this from her will be near damn impossible.

AFTER I HAD BEEN RETURNED TO MY ROOM, I SCRUBBED MY FACE RAW AND TOOK a long, hot shower. I wanted to wash the shame from my body. Every time I closed my eyelids, I saw Jeremy's face, and the look that he had. The look of pure rage when he saw what Jax had dressed me in tonight. I had been humiliated and exposed. I slanted my head downward and wrapped my arms around myself. I couldn't tell you how long I was in there, but fucked up things came across my mind.

JEREMY
past

"NIC, IF YOU DON'T STOP, I SURE AS FUCK WON'T BE ABLE TO."

"I don't want you to stop, ever."

Those words were music to my fucking ears. I lowered my hands from her hair and palmed her waist. My fingers felt her warm skin through her tight leggings. I couldn't wait to get them off of her. I looked down to her heart shaped face and my eyes darted to her mouth. Her teeth worried her bottom lip.

"Then I won't." Nicole gripped my leather cut and pulled me back down to her. My hands immediately slid to her sexy ass and pulled her against me. Our mouths collided. She was as hungry for me as I was for her. I was eager and she was willing, so I took my moment of opportunity. That night when I found her on the bathroom floor shot through my mind. Her limp body laid in a heap. I had no time to react, no time to think, just do. So, I breathed life back into her body. I kissed her frantically.

"Jer," Nicole mumbled my name. I didn't realize the grip I had on her had tightened. I paused. Her eyes were round and glossy. They searched mine for an answer. An answer as to why I was attacking her mouth. I rested my forehead against hers.

"I..." I couldn't even finish my sentence. Fuckin' pussy. Nicole didn't speak, she just did. Taking my hands into hers, she led me down to the sandy beach by the lake. It was more like small pebbles than the smooth sand that you would find on the coasts. She paused in a clear spot and turned to look back at me. The wind left my chest. The look on her face was one I'd make sure to remember for the rest of my life.

Her hands came to the sides of my cut; she tugged it down over my arms and gently laid it on the sand.

"Babe," I started after her, a man's cut wasn't meant to lay on the fuckin' ground.

"Believe me, it will be worth it. I'm pretty sure that piece of leather hasn't had a naked ass on it." She giggled when stripping her top off.

"Well, when you put it like that." I toed off my riding boots and my jeans pooled at my feet. I peered over at Nic. Her tight little ass looked hella good. She bent at the waist to take her black leggings off. The noise that left my throat had her giggling again. And Goddamn, I loved the sound of her laugh.

When we were both down to our underwear, we stood bare chest to bare chest. Nicole's petite hard nipples pressed into my skin. I sat her down on my cut and got down on my knees in front of her. My fingers hooked behind her knees and drew her towards me. The backs of her thighs clashed against the tops of my bent legs. Nicole grasped for the waistband on my briefs as I reached for her panties.

"Slow down, Jeremy," her small hand came to the center of my chest, "I'm not going anywhere."

"You better not be!" I grunted as I slowed my pace. Easier said than done.

Silent, Nicole laid herself down and reached for me. Leaning over her small frame, I leaned on my right forearm as my left hand pulled down my briefs. I half expected to feel her tense underneath me when my dick hit her thigh, but her hips rose upward.

"Anxious?" I teased her as I tugged her panties off.

"Like you haven't been dreaming about this happening for the past umpteen years! I've waited long enough," she said a matter-of-factly. She put her cheek next to mine as her tongue darted out to my ear lobe. Instant gratification.

"Damn, girl. Hold on a minute." I sat back, grabbed the pant leg of my jeans, and took my wallet out for a condom. Tearing it open, I sheathed my now impatient dick, and positioned myself between Nicole's creamy thighs.

I settled my forearms on either side of her head as her hands trailed up my bare back, and over my shoulders to cup my biceps.

The heat that radiated between us kept us warm in the cool summer night. I was ready to spit into the palm of my hand, until the head of my dick grazed her wet folds. She was practically dripping wet, for me. Only me. Perfect.

In one slow motion, I took her. I felt her tense as her muscles stretched around me. Her warmth was a feeling I'd never forget. As soon as I felt Nicole's body relax, the tension in her thighs eased up, causing me to sink further into her wet pussy. The heels of her feet pushed on my ass to bring me all the way into her. I greatly accepted what she gave me. It was all mine: her virginity, her cunt, and her body.

Easing my way in and out of her, I heard her small voice.

"Jer?"

"Yeah?"

"I'm not going to break. If you're going to take my v-card then do it right." I pulled out and put all my weight onto her as I thrust my way deep inside her.

"There," she gasped into my neck as she wrapped her arms around me.

"Right there?" I mimicked my motion.

"Yes. Jer?" She leaned back against the cool ground.

"Yeah, babe?"

"I love you."

And without any hesitation I told her, "I love you too, Nicole."

Well, now I claimed her heart as well. I'm fucked.

CHAPTER 12

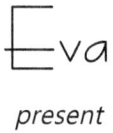va

present

AFTER CLEANING UP THE STAGE AND GETTING THE CLUB GIRLS OUT OF THE clubhouse, I proceeded to make my way towards the boys' rooms. Jax ordered me to take both Derrick and Hunter back to their rooms. The Derrick kid was a total baby-faced lady-killer. If that wasn't an oxymoron, then I don't know what is. It felt cruel bringing him back to his holding room; the kid has some serious fuckin' issues. Although, I could have sworn I saw a chain around his neck, one that looked similar to someone in the service. Tags, maybe. Yum, a man in fatigues, hot! Shaking my head I went to Jax's office, where I was instructed to wait for Hunter while Jax finished up with him.

I heard a pair of boots come down the hallway, and my eyes darted over as I knew that gait anywhere. Jamison, Jax's father.

"There she is." Jamison made his way over to where I stood, leaning up against a wall.

"James." I tipped my chin in his direction; I didn't want him asking why I was loitering by the Chapel.

"Tell my son I said hello. I have some business that needs my immediate attention." Nicole. He must have caught wind that she was here. His baby girl, Nicole. What a fuckin' shit storm. As soon as I could no longer hear Jamison's boots, the door to Jax's office swung open. A pissed off Hunter emerged and his dark eyes bored into mine. It was like time stood still, as the tension between the two of us was what it was that night he found out who I really was. Jax was next, and he sidestepped Hunter and honed in on me.

"Show him to his room, then come to mine." His rough calloused hands followed my jawline. I didn't like the tone in his voice or the sinful look in his eye. Something was wrong, very wrong.

"As you wish," I replied to his command and walked towards the part of the club that was connected to the coke sweatshop, as well as Hunter's room. Hunter- he was dead quiet. I felt his eyes like laser beams cutting into the back of my head. I walked with force as my heels echoed against the faux hardwood floors.

"Silent treatment now?" I asked over my shoulder as I led us.

Nothing.

We walked a little further.

"Still nothing?" I giggled lightly as I turned around and my smile fell as soon as I saw Hunter's face. If looks could kill, consider me six feet under. I halted to a stop, as his eyes seemed to have lit with something. It was a mix of beauty and rage.

"I have nothing to say to you." His jaw flexed under the florescent lighting. My eyebrow cocked itself.

"Good, 'cause I have nothing to say to you either." I went to turn back around and I felt his hands grab me. I was shoved up against the wall.

"Not here, he has camera's on these halls!" I hissed as my shoulder blades slammed against the wall. Before I knew it, Hunter was leading us down the hallway to his room.

"What are you, nuts? What the fuck is the matter with you? You trying to get us both killed?" I unlocked his room and I was hauled inside.

"You have nothing to say to me?!" I was up between a door and a hard place. That hard place being Hunter's jacked body. Sweet Jesus.

"Would you please explain to me what the fuck is going on?"

"How about you tell me what the fuck is going on?"

"What are you tal-." His palms smacked the wall on either side of my head. I had a quick flashback to that night. There is one thing he doesn't know about. That one thing, I'll never give up. Hunter would kill me if he knew the truth.

"DON'T FUCKIN LIE TO ME!" I felt his body shake with adrenaline and fury.

"Stop it!" I shoved at his chest, earning me a few inches of space from him.

"Tell me now, Eva, or I swear to fucking God, that I'll give you up so fast..."

"Are you threatening me? That's funny considering you're the one who's fucked right now. You're the one being held hostage by a rival MC. Jax's father, Jamison, has a lot more in store for you and your brothers. I wouldn't be so worried about what I'm doing. You should be worried about saving your own ass, Sabatino," I shot back at him, shoulders squared.

"That's what I always loved about you, Eva, that mouth. I told you it was going to get you into a shit load of shit one day. And guess what, today is that day."

EVA'S BODY STIFFENED AGAINST ME. SHE WAS PISSED, LIKE I HAD JUST VERBALLY slapped her with my words.

"Hold the fuck up." Here she goes.

"You know, Eva, for being a Fed, you must have excelled in your MC class. You really fucked your way to the top, haven't you?" I verbally spit those words in her beautiful face.

The fire ignited in her eyes.

"Well, I didn't hear any complaints when I was riding your dick!" Instinctively, my hand reached out and my fingertips smacked her mouth. Shocked, Eva put her hands to her lips.

I was pissed at myself for letting her smart ass comment get to me, and for touching her like that. I wasn't that type of man. My mother raised me better. I should have never put my hands on her, but fuck, she knows exactly what to say to get under my skin. I turned my back to her and pushed my hands through my hair.

"I can't believe you just did that."

"No? I can't believe you just said that!" My temper flared again as my right arm flayed about in front of me. Eva backed against the wall. Fuck, she thought I was going to hit her again.

"So what is your problem then? If you're going to be talking all this shit, you better have something to back it up, because I, for one, don't appreciate your bull-fucking-shit." I cut her off right there.

"Were you ever going to tell me?"

"What? Tell you, what?"

"You're fucking kidding me right now, aren't you?" Eva pushed off the wall and stood up to me.

"Kidding you about what, Hunter? Stop with the fuckin' riddles. Was I ever going to tell you about what?" Her red hair swung over her right shoulder as she raised her hand to massage her temple.

"My daughter." The words sounded so foreign coming from my mouth, but fuck, did saying that make my chest swell with pride. I watched Eva's dark eyes go wide, and she froze like ice.

"I-I have to go," Eva stuttered, trying to avoid the situation. She rapidly turned her back to me as she reached for the door handle. I pulled her back against the front of my body. My fingers dug into the flesh on her hips, hips that bared my child. I walked us forward so the front of her body was flush against the door, forcing her face to turn sideways and her cheek to lie alongside the cool metal. As Eva closed her eyes, her sooty eyelashes contrasted against her creamy skin, and now flushed face. No matter how mad I was at her, Eva was beyond gorgeous. Eva was a living and breathing goddess in my book, and I worshiped the shit outta that woman. She was my weakness, *is* and always will be. I can never explain that shit, but it what it is.

"You should have told me." My jaw clenched and the muscles in my cheeks flexed.

"How did you find out?" Her voice came out as a whisper, I barely heard her.

"Does it matter?" I whispered against the back of her head.

"I can't-" She started to pull away from me, but I held tight.

"You can, and you will. How the fuck could you do this? You were going to just live your little lie of a life and never tell your husband that he was a father?"

"Ex-husband."

"Last I checked, you never signed the court papers." She knew I was right. I could see her having a battle within herself. She fought the words that were about to be spoken.

"She's not yours." Eva inhaled a deep breath and looked upward. Her jaw flexed as a tear escaped the corner of her eye. My stomach dropped, but I knew something wasn't right. She was fucking lying through her teeth.

"What the fuck, Eva?" I roared.

"She's not, now let go of me and forget we had this conversation." I eased off of her and let her open the door.

"She has my eyes, smile, hair color, even the dimples." I pointed to my cheeks. "She's beautiful, just like her mother...." My voice faded. The image of that little dark-haired toddler was etched into my mind. I couldn't ever forget the face of an angel, my daughter. A daughter I never knew existed.

"Hunter-" Her voiced cracked.

"At least tell me one thing."

"What's that?" She looked me in the eye. Her brown eyes now brimmed with unshed tears.

"Her name."

"Isabella Rose."

Eva waited for me to say something but I was in shock. She named her after my mother. I went to take a step toward her, but Eva hesitated and walked out, closing and locking the door behind her. If Eva thought my room was soundproof, it wasn't. I heard the cry that she let out as soon as her hand left the doorknob. I kicked the metal chair cross the room and pounded my closed fists and forearms against a wall, hard enough to dent the dry wall. If Jax thought he was going to use my family against me, he was wrong. So fucking wrong.

I FELT THE FIRST TWINGE OF PAIN WHEN HUNTER ASKED ABOUT HIS DAUGHTER, our daughter. The life that we created together and the fatherhood he's been missing out on. I was six weeks pregnant when I was re-assigned to the Devils MC. Yes, I knew, and hell-to-the no was I running back to Hunter and telling him the news. I wouldn't risk my life and my baby's life, just to congratulate him. I had to let the idea of Hunter go, but I knew in my heart that I would always have a piece of him with me.

My job was unaware of my pre-existing condition as I was heading full-throttle into Idaho to spark up a new investigation. Devils MC were totally opposite of the Hell's Rebels and the Condemned Angels, completely ruthless. They stood for everything corrupt, and I was scared shitless putting myself in that situation. However, the person that was now corrupted was myself. To keep my spot next to Jax, I lied. This lie will haunt me till the day I die. I told Jax that Isabella was his. I was early enough in my pregnancy to play off that he got me pregnant. He was a biker and how was he to know a woman's menstrual cycle, or how the timeline played out. He never questioned her dark features- they were close enough to my natural hair color. Hunter didn't seem to know this little part of my lie. If he did, he would have fuckin' killed me back there.

Now, I have to work to keep both parties happy. Jax wouldn't have told Hunter without a reason. I have to face him tonight, and I pray he doesn't bring up his club business.

CHAPTER 13

Nicole

As I laid on the bed, my mind raced. A knock sounded at my door, followed by footsteps. I thought it was Jax, but there was a different presence in the room. Turning my head I saw a man. Just looking at him, I knew. I knew he was my father.

"Nicole." His deep voice filled the room.

I took in the man before me. In his late fifties, about 6'1", stocky build, salt and pepper hair and beard, tan leathery skin, and a worn Devil's MC cut.

"Donor," I greeted as I sat upright.

"I guess I deserve that. The name is Kit." He rubbed the back of his neck as he pulled up the vanity stool and sat down next to my bedside.

"Kit? Well Kit, I don't want to hear what you have to say." Memories flooded my mind of the night I discovered the entire nightmare. He saw my brain working.

"Your Mom...," he started.

"You don't have the fucking right to even speak of her, you son of a bitch!" I pushed off the bed, going toe-to-toe with a man I barely knew.

"You're not the only one hurting here, Nicole. I miss her too, you know? She was the goddamn love of my life, and she's gone because Vince killed her! With his goddamn bare hands." He made fists between us. "If he weren't dead already, it would have been a bullet from my pistol that would have taken his life." He looked tough as nails on the outside, but from his words I could tell he was a broken man. I felt emotions stir deep in my stomach.

"I watched." I turned away from him, crossing my arms across the front of my body.

"What?" He went to reach for my shoulder, but hesitated.

"I watched my father shoot himself! After he told me I wasn't his. I went almost twenty years of my life calling the wrong man Dad. To find out that not only was my family was a lie, but so was I."

"If I could do it all differently, I would, baby girl." His deep voice soothed something inside of me. I didn't want to feel comfort from this man. I wanted him gone.

"Do what differently?"

"Your mom was married to him, not by fate or love, but by force and family tradition. Rosalie met Vince when they were teenagers. Your Grandfather was riding with the Condemned Angels, and his daughter Rosalie had her future already planned for her, to bring in the next generation. Vince and I, we rode together plenty of times, chased tail, killed for one another, hell- he was my brother through patch. I was a part of a chapter that used to run with the CA's. When I caught the eye of Rosalie, she caught the eye of Vince."

"Go on," I encouraged him.

"Her future was already in the hands of the Condemned Angels MC, there wasn't anything I could do. I watched as he honed in on her, and slowly stole her from me. Even when she was his Old Lady, it didn't stop our young love. We had an ongoing affair. You were a product of it, simple as that." He took out a skinny cigar from the pocket of his vest.

"Your Granddad was no idiot, he warned Vince of mine and Rosalie's friendship. That he didn't trust my actions, my respect, or myself for that matter. It was an unspoken forbidden territory."

"How long was it going on for?" I sat down on the bed, cross-legged, facing him.

"During their marriage- the first year or so. Then all of sudden, Rosalie didn't talk to me for weeks. Weeks grew into months. Until one day I got a letter. She told me she was pregnant, the baby was mine, and she needed to do what was right for her. She needed to be safe and keep the MC and Vince happy, and that I should move on with my life.

"But you didn't."

"I couldn't. Seeing her with him, fucking killed me. When I didn't hear from Rosalie for those couple of months, then to find out she was having you, it changed the game- for me at least. I was going to keep fighting for her. For our love. For our child. You. So I wrote her back, saying I wanted to know everything, be involved and know my child. A few days went by, I thought I had truly lost her, but then she wrote me back. And so, we became pen pals. I had Rosalie, one way or another- but in those letters, she gave me everything. Her thoughts, fears, dreams, desires, everything. You name it- we wrote it."

"Eventually you moved on and had another family."

"I did. I met Jade shortly after your mom married Vincent. Ryder was only a few months older than you. I had to go on living my life, Nicole. I couldn't make it obvious that I was back and forth with your mother. Christ, I would have been stripped of my patch and killed right on the spot if Kit knew what was going on."

"Well, he took his anger and hate out on her." Hot tears rolled down my face. The pained look on his face said it all.

"Fucking Christ." He drew in a drag from his cigar and ran his thumbnail across his lip.

"So, the feud between the Devils and the Condemned Angels..." I trailed off.

"It's because of you, baby girl." Tears blurred my vision. This was overwhelming; I couldn't handle all this shit in one night.

"Can I be alone?"

"Yes, but don't think this conversation is over." He stood up.

"That's fine, but keep your son away from me. I'm not into incest."

"What?" Kit's voice boomed throughout the room.

"In case you've been blind, Eva isn't the only one who is keeping Jax's bed warm at night."

"Jesus Christ! He won't be laying a fucking finger on you."

"Too late." I avoided eye contact with him.

Without another word, Kit left me.

CHAPTER 14

CHASE

"So, we have a report from Eli and Wyatt. They are being held in separate rooms. Alive, and as good as they could be I'm sure. There was some interest in Hunter as he was in a meeting with Jax. Who knows what the fuck about."

"Jeremy, where is he?" Morreti was jumping the gun.

"Things with him have been quiet. Nicole as well."

"What do we know about Jax's Old Lady?"

"Don't know. Eli stated that she had been babysitting Hunter for some odd reason. Let me find out if he is working some kind of charm on her. Leave it to him to try and get his dick wet while on his death bed." I chuckled and my brothers soon joined in.

"Well, leave it to him to be thinking with the wrong fucking head. What's their headcount look like? Should we be calling in other chapters to come help?"

"I think we should get backup. They are all carrying guns. There is shift for the perimeter of the clubhouse. Surveillance cameras are all we've been able to spot. There has been a lot of traffic in and out of the place. Maybe drop offs, trades. But our guys are still there."

"Well, let's get in there, wait for shift change to get in. I want to limit the chance of one of our guys getting hit. We need to find them, and get the fuck out of there. If I have to start a Goddamn war, I will. The feud between the Devils and the Condemned Angels ends tonight.

"Agreed." I nodded my head while Moretti slammed down the gavel, not even waiting for confirmation from the other brothers. No vote was needed today at this very moment. We were rolling in deep to retrieve our VP.

JEREMY

I HAD BEEN IN MY ROOM FOR FAR TOO FUCKING LONG. I COULD ONLY IMAGINE what Jax wanted with Hunter. How fucking awkward it would be to talk to the man who's fucking your wife. I needed to focus on Nicole. Fuck all the other shit right now. I had to think of something, and fast. I was getting us the fuck out of here. I heard a pair of heels at my doorway and I expected Eva to waltz right on in. Right about now, I wished it were her.

"Hey there, handsome." Nina's voice filled the small room.

Fucking Christ.

I said nothing as I sat on the chair in my room. This was not what I fucking needed right now. Nina sauntered over to me, wearing skinny jeans and a Devils MC t-shirt that had been sliced across the chest, exposing her big ole' tits. Shit, I should have just steered clear of her pussy. Bad fucking idea that was.

"You got a smoke?" I peered up at her.

"Yeah, I figured you might need that and some other things to help pass the time." Nina pulled a pack of smokes and a lighter from her back pocket. I placed the stick of cancer between my lips, and allowed Nina to light it up. Blowing a cloud of smoke above us, I ran my thumbnail across my lower lip.

"Thanks." I sat down on the edge of my bed, and realized that wasn't a good fucking position to be in. I immediately shot up and walked to the other side of the room.

"You know I don't bite." Her small giggle filled the room. Silent, I gave her the once over. Her blue eyes mirrored Nicole's.

"Look Nina, things were fun before I knew you were a part of the fucking Devils."

"I don't think you'd mind even after knowing that little tidbit. "

"Does your lover...I mean brother know that you're here?" I cleared my throat.

"Maybe." She walked over to where I stood and pressed the front of her body against mine. I gripped her by her biceps.

"Fuck off, Nina. I don't want or need your corrupt pussy anywhere near my dick or me. You best be running along now." She shrugged out of my grip and grabbed my hand to cup her sex. I felt the heat radiating through the crotch of her jeans.

"Mmm, you know you want this again," Nina moaned as she tilted her head back.

"Fuck off." I yanked my hand back.

"Fuck you, Jeremy. You know you'll never get her back. She's a Devil now. You'll never make it out of here alive."

"The fuck I am, you little bitch." I tossed my cigarette to the ground and grabbed her biceps again. I gave her a rough shake. Except, she enjoyed it. Nina liked it rough; she was fucking getting off on this shit. Sick little cunt.

"So while you can, you better get it." Nina leaned forward and licked my lips.

"You know what? You're right." I smirked down at her. I grabbed the crotch of my jeans and stretched it taut with my left hand, and pulled my zipper down with my right. Nina's eyes lit up like a damn Christmas tree. I whipped my dick out and palmed it for a few pumps. Nina licked her lips before starting towards me, until she stopped dead in her tracks. Her eyes grew wide and her gaze shot to the floor. There I was, taking a straight piss on her feet. Her scream filled the room as she jumped back from me. I bent my knee and aimed upward to try and stretch my stream. I was enjoying this way too fucking much. After Nina scrambled out of there, I tucked myself back into my jeans and laughed.

She's a Devil now. Those words got to me more than I'd like to admit. I wasn't going to give up on Nicole. Never again. I came too close, too many times to not getting her back. I should have never let her go in the first place.

past ...

After that night with Nicole, something in me changed. I felt things for her. Feelings I had never experienced with anyone else. I never told Chase about Nicole and I, but he took notice.

"Brother, you doing alright?" He walked up behind me and slapped me on the shoulder as we were sitting in my driveway, polishing the pipes on our bikes.

"Yeah, why?" I asked over my shoulder.

"Don't know. Something happen at the bonfire with you and Nic?" *Fucker.*

"Why would you think that?"

"'Cause the next day when I saw you, you had a shit eating grin," he chuckled, tossing me a fresh rag.

"Well, I guess that you'll never know- quit fishin' for deets."

"Just make sure you keep your head on straight. We have a lot coming up while being Prospects. Our main focus is the club. Not getting wrapped up in that pussy voodoo." I paused. Shit. He was right. Once we really go into our Prospect positions- we were at the club's beck and call for the next year or so until we got patched in. I wouldn't be able to give Nicole what she needed.

The remainder of the day, my mind raced with all of the scenarios. Nicole and Roxy were going to college in a few months.

I heard a car door slam. Nicole was dropping off Roxy from a shopping trip. The girls hauled bag upon bag into the house. I shook my head with a laugh. Chicks and their shit.

"Jer. Chase," Roxy greeted us as she passed. Chase's eyes traveled up. Before they could trail any further upward, I threw my rag at his face. The girls laughed as they continued their way onto the front porch. I pushed off my stool and walked to Nicole. I grabbed the extra polishing rag from my back pocket and starting to wipe my hands. Nicole tossed the shopping bags down and turned towards me.

"Hey." Nicole rocked up on her tiptoes.

"Hey." I smiled down at her.

"You want to stop by later tonight?" Nicole asked in a hushed tone. Only for our ears.

"Yeah. I'll let you know when I'm on my way." Pussy whipped.

later that night...

I pulled up to Nicole's house around nine o'clock. I stood on her porch, regretting what I was about to do. She answered the door wearing yoga pants and an old Condemned Angels MC t-shirt that had the neck cut out and was hanging off her shoulder. I ran my tongue over my bottom lip and made my way over the threshold.

Without a word, I pulled her against me, Nic's backside pressed into my front. I couldn't wait another fucking minute to touch her. To savor what is mine and what always will be mine. A small moan mixed with a sigh came from Nicole. Her body melted into me. I latched onto the dip between her neck and shoulder. I nibbled my way back behind her ear. Nic's arms came up behind her, grabbing a fistful of my hair. The only problem was I couldn't stop thinking.

"Why did you stop?" She turned in my arms and looked up at me.

"Just have a lot of my mind." I rubbed my fingers along her waist.

"You're not regretting the other night are you?" She started to withdraw her arms from around me.

"No, not that, babe." I grabbed her wrists in my hands, and

looked down at our joined hands.

"Then, what is it? You're a Prospect, so you can't have real serious club matters yet." She giggled, but soon stopped when she noticed I wasn't laughing.

"That's just it, Nic."

"I'm confused."

"I'm always going to be there for my club. Now, and down the road."

"Yeah, no shit, Sherlock."

"I think with you going away to school, that it will give you a good opportunity to find someone."

"What the fuck, Jeremy?"

"You deserve better than this, than me. Get you away from all the club bullshit and move on with your life."

"Did you even consider my thoughts or feelings on this stupid ass plan of yours?" Her arms crossed her chest.

"Yeah. I think it's for the best." I rubbed the back of my neck, unable to look into her eyes.

A fake laugh came from her, and she shook her head from side to side. I took the risk and stared into her eyes. Tears were already threatening to fall. I felt like I had been punched in the gut.

"Nic." I reached for her, but she leaned away. Now, she avoided eye contact with me, and she bit the inside of her cheek as tears rolled freely down her face. Fuck- I couldn't stand when females cried, let alone her.

"Just go."

"Let me just-"

"No! You got what you wanted from me, now you can just leave," she shouted at me, while she shoved past me and opened the front door.

"It's not like that, Nic!"

"Yeah, sure. Whatever you say, Jeremy." She was stubborn as fuck, and I should have expected her to throw my ass out.

"I meant what I said that night, just remember that." *I love you.*

"Goodbye." Her eyelids closed, more tears escaped. Pissed off at myself and the entire fucking situation, I stormed past her. Out of her house and out of her life. I had to keep reminding myself that this was what was best for her.

Eva

present

IN JAX'S ROOM, HE HAD ME PLAYING THE WAITING GAME. I WAITED FOR HIM TO finish up with club work, whatever that is. I've been uneasy since Hunter confronted me about Isabella. There is only one way Hunter could have found out about our daughter. Jax. Could he have made the connection between the two? Does he know? I'll be fucking done if he finds out the truth. Before my mind could wander any further, Jax entered our room; his eyes scanned me sitting on our bed. I wore a black tank and cotton booty shorts, Jax's favorite. His blue eyes seemed distant and for the first time in a long time, I couldn't read him.

"Eva." Jax started towards me.

"Jax." I went to crawl off our bed, but he put up his palm to stop me from going any further.

"Let me take a look at you, 'cause damn, sweetheart, you look good tonight." His tongue ran across his bottom lip. I concentrated on his mouth, avoided eye contact at all costs.

"Everything alright, baby?" I sat up on my knees and tugged at his leather cut. I curled my fists into the lapels and pulled him forward. Jax trailed his rough hands up the back of my arms, my skin broke out in goose bumps.

"I've had one fuckin' hell of a day, darlin'." He exhaled deeply as his hands met at the back of my neck.

"Let me help you." My hands moved inside his cut, slowly moving it off his shoulders and off his body. Jax's body language screamed sex. It radiated off his body. His wide shoulders led down to his slim waist. I raked my nails down his back, and grabbed the edge of his

90

shirt. I pulled it upward, stirring his slicked back hair. His hands gripped my tank top.

"So Goddamn beautiful, what a shame." Jax was fixated on my mouth. He leaned down and captured my lips with his. He fisted my hair and gingerly tipped my head back. My mouth somewhat fell open as he kissed my jawline.

"What's a shame?" I whispered into his ear.

"You." My eyes sluggishly opened.

"What are you talking about, Jax?"

"You know how I am, Eva. I'm a very jealous man. What's mine is mine. It's not to be touched by anyone else. It's not supposed to be full of lies. It's not supposed to hide anything. It's not supposed to cross me. It's supposed to obey my every command, and fulfill every wish." His fist tightened around my hair.

"Jax, you're hurting me!" I grabbed onto his wrists.

"You're hurting ME, Eva!" he shouted in my face. He leaned over the bed, bending me backwards. I was lucky to move my legs out from underneath me. Jax got one knee up on the mattress.

"When are you going to stop lying to me and start telling me the truth?"

"Stop it! I don't know what you're talking about!" I bucked my hips upward.

"No? Let's jog your memory." Jax wolf whistled and the door to our bedroom slammed open. The door bounced off the back wall and two prospects dragged in something. They came closer. They were dragging not something, but someone. Hunter. Each of the prospects had Hunter's arms linked with theirs. His head hung low as he was dragged in on the tips of his boots.

"What are you doing?" I avoided looking at Hunter and the limp heap he was in.

"Bring him closer," Jax demanded as he pulled me off the bed. My knees hit the ground with a thud. I tried to cooperate, and move in the direction of where he was pulling me in. He brought me right in front of Hunter. The prospect gripped Hunter's short hair and yanked his head back. I gasped in shock. Hunter had been beaten. I could see a busted eyebrow, lip, and a bruised cheek. Hunter moaned in pain, as his eyes focused on me.

"I don't understand," I cried out when Jax slapped me across the face. Hunter strained against the men holding him.

"He does, why don't you?" Jax pointed back to Hunter. My watery eyes glimpsed over to Hunter. Jax released his grip on me and walked up to Hunter. He gripped his chin and punched Hunter, just to line him up for another shot. Three hits in, I couldn't take it.

"Stop! Stop it!" I screamed out.

"Maybe this will help you understand." Jax whistled again.

CHAPTER 15

Nicole

AFTER KIT LEFT, I FELT NUMB. I FELT COMFORTED BY HIS STORY. I FELT LIKE WE connected in some weird way. I mean, I know I am his daughter and all, but I felt a connection that I haven't felt since my parents were alive. It's wild to think that Kit and my mother's story seemed romantic. Like an MC fairy tale gone wrong. A gunshot broke the silence. I shot up off my bed. *What the fuck is going on?*

It sounded like World War III was happening out there. I quickly threw on my combat boots- ready to kick some ass, or whoever the fuck was about to come through my door. I grabbed the small stool that sat at my vanity. There was a gunshot and a thud outside my door. I jumped and tightened my grip on the wood legs. This little ass thing better save my life, or I'll be pissed. There were voices that I couldn't make out. Keys jingled in the door and I positioned myself behind the door. I brought my arms above my head, and the first person into my room I swung at. They went down hard, with their hand gripping the back of their head. I went in for another swing; with the cylinder of wood I had remaining. Men shouted and started to go for the man on the ground.

"Fuck!" I would know that voice anywhere.

"Jer?" My arm paused overhead.

"Nic? What the fuck, baby!" He looked up at me from the ground. He caught a glance of his palm, and thank God, I didn't cause any real damage.

"Oh God, Jeremy!" I threw myself into his arms as soon as he sat back on his haunches, tipping us both over on the ground. It felt like fucking years since I've touched him. Jeremy stroked my hair, and pulled my face back to look at me. As soon as my eyes hit his, his mouth claimed mine. His short and soft beard grazed my skin as his lips worked over mine. My body inched up on his as I fisted his cut.

"Alright, alright, you two. Break it up. Save that shit for later." Chase gripped Jeremy's shoulder and pulled him upward, bringing me with him.

"See if I ever come between you and Rox, you fucker." Jeremy drew me against his chest.

"We have got to move. We need to keep moving, get Derrick!" Moretti's voice boomed in our room. The hallway lights were halfway shot to shit; the door across from mine was open.

"I was here, across the hall from you. All this time?" I slowed down as I glanced into his room.

"Not now, Nic, we have to get the boys and get the fuck out of here. Take this." Chase dropped a handgun in to my hands. The men watched me as I looked down at the weapon. I checked the chamber and cartridge. After I palmed the cartridge back into the handle, I looked up at surprised eyes.

"What?" I shrugged them off. Yes, this woman has packed heat before. Fuckin' men.

"Where is Derrick? I'll start down here, we meet in the middle." I waved my gun down the right wing of the dimly lit hallway. Jeremy started on the doors opposite of me.

CHAPTER 16

Nicole

"D?" I UNLOCKED THE DOORS AS I WENT, JEREMY JUST KICKED IN THE DOORS ON his side of the hallway.

I heard shuffling and a clanking noise from the bathroom, and I barged through the doorway. Just as I rushed through the door, there was Derrick with his handcuffed wrists wrapped around a ceramic toilet. He stood up from a squat, with interlaced fingers around the back of the bowl. His strength pulled the toiled off the ground, and the links on his cuffs broke apart. Water sprayed everywhere. Derrick was drenched. His white t-shirt became transparent, and his bulging muscles and inked chest appeared through the wet fabric.

"Derrick?" I tried to get him out of the "hulk trance" he was in. His head turned toward me- his dark eyes were threatening and fierce. He charged at me, shoved me against the bathroom doorframe. His body went flush against mine. Derrick's hands caressed my face; blood and water trickled down his wrists.

"Reese?" I barely heard him over the water spraying. *Reese? Why would he be calling for her?*

"Brother, back off her." Jeremy was at my side, he gripped Derrick by the shoulder and tugged him away from me. The front of my shirt and jeans were soaked.

"What happened?" Derrick shook his head, and he seemed to come back from his trance.

"You with us?" Jeremy gripped the back of his neck.

"Yeah, let's go." Derrick stared at me. His eyes said it all. He knew what I heard. Yet, I didn't say a word.

We quickly gathered Derrick and the three of us made our way down the original hallway. Jeremy called out to the others so we could move to get Hunter.

HUNTER

BEFORE I WAS BROUGHT TO EVA, JAX PAID ME A VISIT, HIM AND HIS PUSSY brothers. He let those motherfuckers take their good ol' time taking their rounds of pounding on me. My ribs fucking killed, my face was numb and swollen. Jax just stood against the doorframe and watched as I took my beating. I knew exactly the reasoning behind it. My girls. It took me a few minutes to realize that they stopped. My body went limp against the cold cement ground, now splattered with my blood.

"Hunter, is it?" Jax's voice filled the small room.

"Yeah, you mother fucker?" I spit out the blood collecting in my mouth.

"I want to show you something. Or maybe even teach you rather."

"What could you possibly teach me?" I grunted as I rolled to my side and cradled my ribs on my left side.

"I want you to know what you've missed since you let Eva go. Know what you'll never have. And if you ever touch her again, I'll kill you myself."

"Go ahead, do what you feel like you need to do to take care of your insecurities. Sounds to me like you have some real trust issues." I chuckled as my fist pushed off the ground and I gradually sat back on my heels.

"Bring him!" Jax demanded, and my elbows were gripped before I collapsed into their hold. The next time I came around, I was in a different room. My eyes, or at least the one that wasn't swollen shut, blinked. My vision came into focus. Eva stood before me, with Jax's grip on the back of her neck as he tossed her to the floor in front of me.

"I don't understand," Eva pleaded, only to be slapped across the face by Jax. A surge of adrenaline pumped through my veins as I struggled against the men who held me. I was going to destroy that fucker. Eva's small hand cupped her red check. Before I knew it, he headed my way and laid out his punches. I could hear Eva's pleas in the background. I groaned as Jax's fist stopped mid-air, with Eva holding him back.

"Stop it! Stop it!" she screamed at him. Jax shrugged her off and whistled to his men. Signaled them for something. Before I knew what had happened, a pair of shoes came into my line of sight. I glanced over; there were a petite pair of black Vans. My gaze drifted upward and saw a head full of thick, unruly black hair. The same color hair as mine. The little girl stood a little taller than me on my kneeling knees. She wrung her hands nervously as two men guided her by her shoulders. She caught a sideways glimpse of me. Those eyes. My eyes. Isabella.

"I swear to God, Jax," Eva cried out as she clung to his leg.

"You'll do nothing, Eva!" Jax shouted back at her. Isabella jumped next to me.

"Daddy, stop it!" God love her, Isabella stomped her foot as her little fist flayed about. But fuck me, hearing her call Jax, Daddy, ripped my heart to shreds.

"Come here, baby." He crouched down on his haunches.

"She isn't a part of this, please, Jax. Just leave her out of this." Eva's voice cracked slightly. He gave her a glimpse over his shoulder.

"Don't tell me what to do with my own daughter." I couldn't help but to chuckle at that. I already felt Eva's eyes on me before I even lifted my head.

"Care to enlighten me, Hunter?" Jax encouraged Isabella to stand behind him, and toward her mother. My focus was now on the two of them. Isabella was the perfect combination of the both of us. She had my hair, and eyes. Her fair skin, heart- shaped face, and full dimpled cheeks were her mother's. She was beautiful. I could tell that she had Eva's spunk. *My girls.* Something in me snapped. I don't know if it was my pent up frustration with Eva and her lies, or the smug as shit look on Jax's face, the fact that my brothers and I have been held in this pisser of a club, or that I've been beaten. I think that's one too many fucking reasons for my next action. Clearly, I couldn't take back the next set of words to leave my mouth.

"Your daughter?" I sneered at him.

"Hunter," Eva cut me off. I glanced over at her. Tears brimmed her big round eyes. She shook her head from side to side, silently pleading for me to stop. But fuck it; my mouth wasn't functioning when I heard another man claim my daughter as his own. Not today, you fucker. Jax glanced at Eva as soon as my name left her mouth. Her eyes darted back to Jax, pleading.

"What is he saying?" His hand curled around Isabella's small arm. I thrashed against the two men holding me.

"Nothing. He's saying nothing." Eva hurried her words.

"Tell him, Eva." I encouraged her. Time to come clean, baby.

ACKNOWLEDGEMENTS

MANY THANKS TO MY OTHER HALF, JON. YOU HAVE BEEN SO PATIENT THROUGH all my takeovers, writing sessions, PicMonkey creations, and more. You pushed me to stop reading, and WRITE all of those nights, while you entertained Sofia. Thank you for your support and pushing to me to continue and reach my goals. I couldn't have done this without you.

Mandy- you and the team at Raw Books are amazing. You never let me down, and always help me grow and learn. I can only hope that I've gotten better through this series. Ha! But, seriously- you rock and I can't say how much I appreciate your help, constructive criticism, and advice. It's helped, greatly.

Brenda, thank you for being the lucky lady to make this steamy cover! You know I had to take it back to tats and nipple piercings haha. I can't wait to reveal Dark Paradise's cover with everyone.

Max Henry- girl you rock my world. I can't wait to show off this bad boy after you've gotten your talented hands on the book. You make it all come to life and give all my books the facelift they need.

My Beta readers- you ladies are AMAZING, and I greatly appreciate you making time in such short notice- you are fantastic

Love Between the Sheets for hosting my Blitz and Blog Tour, Mary- what would I do without you?

My Street Team, Heather's Hell Raisers- you ladies are simply fantastic, thank you for your dedication, time and loyalty.

Amy Donnelly, thank you thank you thank you, for all your support, advice, help, creative ideas, and graphic designs. I can't wait for our author event and the projects ahead of us!

The readers- I couldn't do this without you. You've been awesome. Helping me mold myself and letting me know what you want, like, love, hate. I can say that writing has been so much fun and I love making people happy, get an escape for a few hours, and make them laugh. I hope you liked Reckless Abandon and will look forward to Dark Paradise.

Tell Me What You Think

What would you like to happen in the next part of the
Condemned Angels MC Series???

I appreciate feedback and comments to see what you thought!

Send me a direct **email**:
heatherleighbooks@gmail.com

Find me on **Goodreads**:
www.goodreads.com/author/show/8056685.Heather_Leigh

Like me on **Facebook**:
www.facebook.com/HeatherLeighBooks

Follow me on **Twitter**:
Author Heather Leigh
@HLeighBooks

COMING SOON

Condemned Angels # 4

HEATHER LEIGH